Friends, and Other Perishables

Friends, and Other Perishables

Dale Whisman

Five Star • Waterville, Maine

Copyright © 2004 by Dale Whisman.

All rights reserved.

This novel is a work of fiction. Names, characters, places and incidents are either the product of the author's imagination, or, if real, used fictitiously.

No part of this book may be reproduced or transmitted in any form or by any electronic or mechanical means, including photocopying, recording or by any information storage and retrieval system, without the express written permission of the publisher, except where permitted by law.

First Edition
First Printing: December 2004

Published in 2004 in conjunction with Tekno Books and Ed Gorman.

Set in 11 pt. Plantin by Myrna S. Raven.

Printed in the United States on permanent paper.

Library of Congress Cataloging-in-Publication Data

Whisman, Dale.
   Friends and other perishables / by Dale Whisman.—1st ed.
     p. cm.
   ISBN 1-59414-259-9 (hc : alk. paper)
    1. Private investigators—Fiction. 2. Insurance crimes—Fiction. 3. Male friendship—Fiction. 4. Informers—Fiction. I. Title.
   PS3623.H56F75 2004
   813'.6—dc22   2004042396

I dedicate this book and my life
to my beloved wife, Sherry.
Her patience, and understanding have made
both possible.

CHAPTER ONE

I stood over him, my fingers clamped around the butt of the .45, shaking so badly I knew if I tried to holster the damn thing I'd drop it. The rain had almost stopped, but the runoff flowed over my shoes as it washed Jimmy's blood into a nearby sewer drain. I kept thinking of useless things, like CPR and dialing 911, all the time looking down at a hole in his forehead I could shove my thumb into.

Jimmy was no gunman. As far as I knew he had never owned a gun in his life—maybe never fired one before tonight. If I had been able to see well enough in the dark to recognize who was shooting at me, I might never have killed him.

I walked to the mouth of the alley, wondering if anyone had called the cops. My ears were still ringing from the noise. It wouldn't be the first time shots had gone unreported in the area. I was playing with the idea of just walking away, but it had been a justifiable shooting and I am licensed to carry the automatic. Besides, my arm was starting to hurt like hell. I was going to need a doctor. My cell phone, the little one that fits in your pocket so you'll always have it with you, was still in my van. I started walking back down the street just as a squad car turned the corner, flashing red and blue lights mirrored in the wet pavement.

Right there I could have become the late Carl Jacobs, because the Colt was still in my hand, and Tulsa cops answering a "shots fired" call on a rainy Saturday night are in no mood to take chances. My luck held. Between them these two probably had thirty years experience. They didn't jump out of the patrol car and shoot me. The driver stepped out slowly, crouched behind the door, and took command. "Drop the weapon. Now!"

I thumbed on the safety, held my right foot out slightly, and dropped the automatic so that it hit my shoe before crashing into the concrete.

His voice was calm and steady as he called out instructions to me. "Hands on top of your head, lace your fingers. Turn around, face away from me. Now back toward my voice, slowly. Stop there. Drop to your knees."

He didn't threaten or explain what would happen if I didn't do exactly what he said. The implication was in his voice. He was thorough and professional, and I had no doubt his partner was in a position to drop me if I made a wrong move. It was a little difficult for me to get down on my knees without using my hands. I managed, and found myself kneeling in a pool of cold rainwater that soaked through my slacks, sending goose bumps up my back. Of course, a few of those bumps, and the chill I was feeling, may have been the result of shock because of my wound. More than likely, it was just delayed fear. Until tonight I hadn't been shot at in quite a long time.

The driver was quiet as he approached me. I never knew he was there till I felt him grip my linked fingers firmly in his left hand. He holstered his pistol and slipped the cuffs first on my right wrist, which he forced down to the small of my back. When he twisted my left arm around to bring my wrists together, the pain in my shoulder grew more insistent. Before they allowed me to stand, he went through a search routine, squeezing pockets, waistband, ankles, and wrists. Not patting, the way Joe Friday used to do it. Patting would have found my automatic if it had been stored away in the Milt Sparks waistband holster. Patting would not have found the slim little Italian switchblade knife I carry inside my shirt suspended from a string around my neck. It rides in the chest hollow below my tie. I've practiced using two fingers, reaching in between shirt buttons to pull it free. He managed without any practice, and his expression made clear his opinion of people who carried knives. At least he didn't hit me.

"Officer, my name is Carl Jacobs. I'm a licensed Private Investigator. I have a permit for the pistol. My identification and license are in the wallet."

"Yeah? You got a permit for the switchblade?"

"It's an antique, a collector's item." Lame, but it was the only excuse I could think of.

"Used to be your mama's, I guess. You flinched when I cuffed you, and you got blood on your overcoat. You hurt, or have you left a victim lying around somewhere?"

"Both. I've got a bullet in my left arm, and there's a DOA in the alley with four of my slugs in him."

He didn't even look in that direction. He held my unopened wallet in his hands, waiting, keeping his eyes on me as the other officer picked up my automatic on his way to the alley. After a moment his partner called out, "It's like the man says, Coop, there's a stiff in here with a hole in his forehead and a .38 Special in his right hand."

"Call it in, Doug. Get a crew down here. Mr. Jacobs, you are under arrest."

He recited the Miranda without referring to the little card he no doubt had in a pocket somewhere, and after I admitted I understood my rights, he asked, "Do you wish to give up these rights and answer my questions?"

"Sure. I'll pass on the attorney for now, but I could use a doctor."

He yelled at Doug to request an ambulance, then turned

back to me, a little puzzled. "You're the coolest bastard I've run into for a long time."

"I'm clean on this. It was an ambush. That's Jimmy Jay in there. You know him?"

"The Blue Jay? Sure. He's a snitch, used to be on payroll to half the cops in the damn city. Lately his information is worth a little less than nothing. Nobody's trusted him in months." His tone implied I must have known about Jimmy's declining reputation.

"Nobody but me. Jimmy called me earlier this evening. Said he had a name and address for me, a name I need in a case I'm working. I was supposed to pick him up on the corner. He was asking fifty bucks, enough to make me think he had something worthwhile. I arrived on time but he wasn't anywhere in sight. Someone called to me from the alley and I crossed over. He started shooting before I ever saw him, and I caught one in the shoulder."

"Why believe him? He's been living on food stamps 'cause his sources dried up long ago."

"Jimmy and I grew up together. He's . . . he was two years younger than me. I've been big all my life, he was always little and skinny. I had to pull his ass out of the fire about once a week when we were kids. He was grateful, and I could count on him to come through for me, at least till tonight."

"So, he was a friend. Why would he try to pop you?" he asked, with much skepticism.

"I didn't say he was a friend. As a kid he was helpless, it was like taking care of a pet. As a man he was a pain in the ass. He used people the way people use paper towels. I never knew him to even carry a gun, let alone use one. He had nothing against me personally, as far as I know, but if he was as bad off as you say, he would have sold me pretty cheap. He probably would have felt bad about it for a whole day or two."

"What went down here?" he said, aiming a thumb toward the dark alley.

"I hate to admit it, but when I walked over here my overcoat was buttoned. He got off five rounds before I could get my automatic free. I fired four times; the last one caught him in the forehead. It's a .45 caliber Colt, loaded with semi-jacketed hollow-points. The medical examiner should testify that after Jimmy took the first round or two in the chest he couldn't blink an eyelid, let alone fire a revolver. That'll show he fired first. They'll bitch about overkill, me pulling off four rounds when one or two would have been enough, but what-the-hell, I was scared."

His partner called out from the squad car as sirens sounded in the distance. "He checks out, Coop. Valid ticket, good reputation downtown. He's cooperated with the department on a couple of occasions, and the word is to give him the benefit of the doubt, as long as it looks like he's being straight with us. But he's not considered untouchable."

"Okay. Tape off the area before those clowns get here. Jacobs, the cuffs stay on till we take your statement downtown and see how it reads. First we'll get your arm treated, but you can plan on being in custody for the rest of the night. Understand?"

"You got it," I agreed, readily.

He paused, staring intently at my face, then asked, "What was your father's name?"

It was so unexpected it took a minute for me to respond. "His name was Carl Jacobs, too. Why?"

"So, you're Carl, Junior?"

"No. His middle name was William. Mine is Brandon.

He always said he didn't want me to grow up as a Junior. Did you know him?"

"Yeah. I knew him. I remember hearing him mention you a few times. And two daughters, right?" I nodded. "I hear he died peacefully, in bed. That so?"

"Yes. He died too young."

"The good ones always do." He looked at his feet for a moment, then said, "I won't report the switchblade, but you don't get it back. I've been stabbed twice. I hate knives, and I don't like guys who carry them."

Three more squad cars arrived before the ambulance. By the time they finally transported me, still in police custody, my arm had gone from minor pain to major agony. At Riverside Hospital emergency room the bandaging was relegated to a bored, skinny intern with bad breath. There was one good-looking nurse on duty, but she was busy trying to chew gum without spilling her coffee. The intern insisted I take the shot of pain killer in the butt instead of my arm, which seemed a little silly to me, but by then I was lightheaded and I could have been wrong. I had been wrong about the bullet; it went all the way through. The exit wound wasn't as bad as it might have been, but a lot of foreign matter from my coat had been driven into the wound. The intern warned me to watch for infection. He wanted to keep me overnight, but I talked him out of it. I think the nurse smiled at me as I was leaving, but she might have been looking at the cop leading me out.

At the station house downtown they asked the same questions over and over again, then left me alone in an interrogation room with a cup of coffee, at which point they forgot all about me. The painkiller kicked in and I was asleep before the coffee was cold. A Homicide Detective I had met a year ago during the Hoskins investigation woke me up about an hour later. He said they were willing to call it self-defense unless further evidence indicated otherwise. I was free to leave. I flagged a taxi out front and gave the driver my home address on East 83rd Street. That meant I would be leaving my van at the scene of the shooting, but the painkiller still had me drowsy, and I was in no shape to drive.

The house was dark and quiet as I let myself in. I stopped in the kitchen for a long swallow of cold milk to soothe my ulcer, then went upstairs to the bedroom. I put the empty holster away in a dresser drawer and undressed slowly, leaving my clothes where they dropped. As I slipped under the covers Sherry stirred, rolled toward me, and without opening her eyes reached out and pulled me to her.

"So, shamus, where have you been all night?" The sleepy warmth in her voice, and seeing her face framed by the soft tangle of dark hair suddenly made me think about dying, and never being able to hold her again.

"I've been out wooing dragons and slaying maidens."

"You're falling down on the job, Mister. You've got a maiden right here at home that needs slaying on a regular basis."

She pressed closer and rested her head on my shoulder. Her cheek brushed against the bandage. Suddenly the sleep was gone from her voice.

"What the hell is that?"

"It's just a little bandage. I got nicked tonight. It's nothing, really."

"Nicked how, with what?"

"Someone took a shot at me." I could feel her stiffen and pull away. "He almost missed entirely. I hardly felt it. Nothing more than a scratch."

Her voice was low and intense, as she glared at me in the

dim light. "You've been home maybe ten hours out of the last three days. The girls and I have to study your picture to be sure we don't let a stranger into the house by mistake. So when you get yourself shot, you don't bother to call and let me know; you go off to some emergency ward, get bandaged up, and drop by the next time you're in the neighborhood? Is that about right?"

"Sherry, I promise you, it's not serious. It happened late last night. I knew you and the girls would be asleep. I expected to be home in a couple of hours. It took longer to give my statement to the cops than I expected. They finished with me an hour ago and I came straight home."

She rolled onto her side and curled up tight. She didn't want me to see, but I knew she was crying. Her voice was muffled by her arms.

"Try to get some sleep. We're supposed to go watch Pam ride this afternoon. Will you be okay?"

"Sure. Wake me up about eleven."

After a short silence, she asked, "Who shot you?"

"It was Jimmy."

"Jimmy Jay? But you and Jimmy . . . Why?"

"I don't know yet."

"Did you ask him? Didn't he give you a reason, for God's sake?"

"No. He didn't say anything. I shot back. He was dead before I knew who he was."

She looked back over her shoulder at me, a sadness in her face. She didn't speak again as she stretched an arm across my chest and cried quietly against my shoulder while I fell asleep. I didn't even have time to wonder what the hell I was going to do next.

CHAPTER TWO

Sherry let me sleep till almost noon. When I finally crawled out of bed I reluctantly decided to settle for a bath, rather than a shower, in order to keep my bandaged arm dry. Then Sherry entered the bedroom with a length of plastic wrap, which she used to cover the bandage. She's been anticipating my needs for over ten years.

As she stood quietly beside me, securing the plastic with a piece of tape, I again marveled at the differences in us. I am a full twelve inches taller than her five-two. I am fair and blonde, while she has the black hair and olive complexion of her Mediterranean ancestors. She has gypsy eyes. Sherry can charm you with a demure sigh, but cross her, and she can blister paint with obscenities. She has mellowed somewhat, having two impressionable young daughters in the house, yet the fire is there, and its warmth keeps me close.

"Carl, before you come down, please put on a long-sleeve shirt." She apparently hadn't said anything to the girls about my wound.

"I will," I assured her.

A slow shower and a quick shave made me feel somewhat better, though the arm was stiff and painful. I sat on the edge of the bed, needing to rest my forty-year-old body between socks, and then between shoes. Might have been due to the wound. Probably it was just old age getting an early start.

Wearing dark slacks, dress shirt, and house shoes, I went downstairs to the living room. The Sunday paper was on the table next to my chair. There wouldn't be anything in it about the shooting, since it happened too late to make the deadline, but it was probably going to be on local news, which was a good reason for not turning on the television. As I put my feet up and opened the paper, eight-year-old Pamela came in from the kitchen with my first cup of coffee. She rested her hand lightly on my shoulder as she put the cup down.

"Hi," she said, brushing my cheek with a fleeting kiss, and moving to the end of the couch closest to me.

"Good morning, Pam. You ready for the big day?" She was wearing her riding habit.

"Yeah, I think so."

"Just a little nervous?"

"No. Maybe a little. It's no big deal."

"Want part of the paper?"

"Sure, thanks."

"Where's your sister?"

"She went to church with the Carsons. She'll be back pretty soon."

We both settled back to read, me with the headlines, Pam with the magazine section. She is a tiny feminine version of me: my hair, my green eyes, even my disposition, God help her. Her lovely face was more often than not masked in a serious, noncommittal expression. I suspect her of hiding her amusement at the rest of us. On those rare occasions when she does laugh, her eyes crinkle and her face brightens. This morning, however, she seemed distracted.

Sherry called me to the kitchen, explained that she and the kids had eaten earlier, and placed before me a perfect cheese omelet with hash browns and buttered toast. She busied herself at the sink, washing dishes while I ate. The won't take chances. I won't do stupid things that'll get me shot. I mean, not again. Not like last night, I mean." My stumbling around got us both to laughing, and she turned in my arms to kiss me, following up with a bite on the lip.

As so often happens, we were interrupted by an offspring. Julie burst through the backdoor, a swirl of energy and giggles and tangled limbs. A year younger than her sister, she was taller by an inch, and very proud of it. She carried her heart in her hands, offering it to everyone. She had her mother's hair and eyes, as well as her feminine charm, which she used shamelessly on everyone who could possibly give her something she absolutely positively had to have, or "just die."

"My turn. My turn." She threw herself at me. In self defense I caught her in my arms, heroically ignoring the stab of pain in my left arm, and kissed her hello. "It's about time you spent some time at home, Daddy," she scolded. "We need a man around the house. Daddy, can I have a new sweater for school? Gayle got one at Miss Jackson's that I could just die for, and she says they're having a sale on sweaters that are too cool. I don't really have many sweaters, and it is starting to get colder, and if I catch cold this winter I'll probably miss school and my grades . . ."

Sherry rescued me, sending Julie upstairs to change clothes, and me outside to warm up the station wagon. We were to spend the afternoon near Bixby, at a riding academy where Pam took lessons. Her class was putting on a special show for the parents, so they might see what their money had bought. I wasn't too concerned about Pam's learning to ride, I already knew the money had been well spent. Those rare moments when her face lit up most often occurred when she was on the back of a horse. Julie had yet to find her passion, though we had seen her sounds of running water and glasses clinking together comforting.

"Sherry, do you know what's bothering Pam?"

"Why, did she say something?"

"No. But she never does. It's little things. Maybe n imagination."

"I think you're right, something is bothering her. Sherry sounded as though something was bothering her, too.

"What is it? Did she get into trouble of some kind?"

Sherry dried her hands, pulled out a kitchen chair, and sat next to me. "I know what it is, but Carl, we can't say anything to her about it. At least not directly. I don't want her to think I was snooping. I was putting some things away in her dresser and I found a newspaper article she had cut out. I remembered reading it over a week ago. It was about the private investigator who was killed. I think she's worried about you, especially when you're away from home for a while."

"Yeah, that was Philip Foster. He probably asked the wrong people too many wrong questions and forgot to duck. He was careless and stupid. Hell, he wore loafers because he wasn't smart enough to tie his own shoes."

"Platitudes don't mean a damn thing to an eight-year-old girl, Carl, or to me either. We're both afraid her daddy is going to get his balls blown off," she said, as she went back to washing dishes, the clinking sounds a little louder. I finished eating and carried my dishes over. Pausing behind her, I put my arms around her and kissed her neck.

"Sherry, I'm sorry. I don't want to worry you. Try to remember that I'm good at my job, I've been doing it for a long time. If you'll have a little faith in me, I promise I through gymnastics, piano lessons, and ballet. I think her satisfaction was in the search and in prying concessions out of her parents. I was living in a house with three women, and the pressure was sometimes exhausting. On the other hand, I couldn't imagine living without them.

The day was a complete success, the weather clear and brisk, and throughout the intricate group maneuvers around and around the large indoor arena, Pam stayed on top of the horse, much to her sister's disappointment. We lingered at the academy looking at horses for a while, and on the way home we stopped at a McDonald's for dinner. We also stopped at a pharmacy to have my painkiller prescription filled, but the girls thought I was getting vitamins.

After an evening of less than inspiring television, Sherry sent them to bed, and we entered into that favorite of all times, our quiet moments together, sprawled on the couch listening to the sounds of fussing, laughter, and whispers from upstairs gradually subside.

Sherry had something on her mind, as did I, but she found the words first. "Let's talk."

"OK."

"I'm not stupid, Carl, you should know that by now."

"I do." And I did.

"And I'm not a timid, frightened piece of fluff, to be protected and sheltered from harm. I can be as tough as any man, and can face up to danger. Maybe I can't laugh at it, but I can cuss it."

"I know that," I said, smiling.

She sat up, turned and watched me closely as she spoke, her voice soft. "Today before we left, I saw you through the window as you raised the hood of the station wagon and looked inside. On the way to the academy you took two wrong turns and had to go around the block to get us back on the right road. Before we left the academy you looked under the hood again, acting like you were checking the oil. When we got home you turned the headlights off before we pulled into the driveway, and when you got to the door you pretended to fumble with the door key so you could examine the lock."

She paused and breathed deeply, before asking the question she had been building up to. "Carl, what was the shooting about last night? Is it over with, or are you . . . all of us, still in danger?"

I sat for a moment, thinking. She didn't rush me, she knew I would be honest with her. I had to straighten it out in my own mind.

"I've been thinking about it all day. Jimmy didn't have a reason in the world to want me dead, not a personal reason, anyway. Someone hired him, or pressured him into it. Well, we don't have to be concerned with Jimmy anymore. He's dead." It came out a little harsh. She flinched slightly and took my hand in hers. "But if someone wanted me dead last night, they still must want it today, and I haven't the slightest idea who it would be."

"What are you working on right now? Still the Jennings girl?" Norma Jennings, the teenage daughter of a local bank director, had disappeared. Her friends were saying she ran off with a thirty-two-year-old Black drug dealer known on the street as Peppermint. Mr. Jennings, embarrassed that his little girl preferred a Black drug pusher over her Caucasian, drug-using friends, had hired me to find her and persuade her to go home.

"That's why Jimmy called me last night. He said he had Peppermint's real name, and address. Now it looks like he fed me that story to get me to meet with him. I can't see any motive for getting rid of me, tied to my looking for the girl, or even the pusher. Hell, he's not a major dealer. He's a punk, feeding his own habit."

"What else?"

"There's nothing. I finished two cases for your boss, turned in the reports a couple of weeks ago. I've been hoping to hear from him again. My calendar is free."

"Oh, damn, that reminds me, I was supposed to tell you to stop by the office tomorrow. Mr. Kellogg does have a couple of cases for you. Surveillances, I think. He told me Friday, but I forgot."

"Are they your cases?" I asked, since I always felt a little uncomfortable working on cases Sherry was trying to settle. We didn't always agree.

"No, they were assigned to Andy Baker. He recommended settlement on both of them, but when Mr. Kellogg read the particulars he decided to delay payment and have you investigate. I swear I don't know why they keep Baker. The son-of-a-bitch has the brain of a demented dachshund. If I did some of the things he's done, they'd can me."

"Not a chance. They need you to make the coffee every morning."

That sent her off on a tirade about coffee, chauvinistic men, and the need for castration as an acceptable punishment. It was several minutes before she remembered her concern about our safety and got back to the point. "Tell me the truth, Carl. I need to know if I should be frightened for you and the girls."

"No, I don't think so," I assured her. "I've just been going through the motions: checking the car, and watching for tails. It's not a bad habit to get into."

"What about the police? What are they doing about it?" she wondered.

"Well, right now I imagine a few of them are thinking it was something personal between Jimmy and me that I haven't told them about. In fact, if it wasn't for the hole in my arm, they probably would have kept me locked up for a while. Other than that, I doubt that any of them are taking it very seriously." I knew when it came out that I shouldn't have said it.

"Well, they damn well better take it seriously. What the hell do they think their job is, if it isn't trying to keep citizens from being murdered? Can't you tell them to keep someone out front? A . . . a stakeout . . . or something? Shouldn't they be protecting you . . . us?"

"Do you really think I should ask them for protection?" I asked, knowing she just needed time to think it over.

She took several deep breaths, ran her fingers through her hair a few times, then, slowly, shook her head. "No, I guess not. You're a licensed investigator. That's what you do. You can't very well go running to the police just because . . . I guess that would be bad for business wouldn't it? And you're too damn proud to ask for help, even if it gets you . . ."

"I'm not going to get shot. I told you, I'm good at my job. And you saw today how careful I'm being, especially where you and the girls are concerned. I said I was just going through the motions, and I think that's all it is, but I am being careful, and I don't want you to worry."

She curled up on my lap and put her arms around my neck, her face buried against my chest. She told me once years ago, just after we were married, she liked to press her ear against my chest and listen to me talk. "You keep going through the motions, shamus. You look for bombs, check for tails, and cover your butt. If you need an extra bodyguard, you call on me."

"You got it, killer," I said, and carried her halfway up the stairs before my arm gave out and I had to ask her to walk the rest of the way. Her laughter almost spoiled the mood.

CHAPTER THREE

Monday morning was hectic, as usual, with Sherry getting the kids ready for school and herself ready for work. At some point during previous years the chore of making toast, setting the breakfast table, and putting out an assortment of cereal boxes fell to me. Since I work out of an office at home, I don't have to jump up and get bathed and dressed in time to leave the house by 7:00 A.M., like everyone else.

Sherry uses the station wagon to drop the girls off at her mother's place, a short walk from the private school they attend. She then drives to an underground parkade downtown, which services the Underhill offices. I never deliver the girls, and I never pick them up. Years ago Sherry's dad had selected a husband for her, the son of a business associate. After she married me against her parents' wishes, neither of us saw or spoke to them, until after Pam was born. They made up with Sherry so they could see their granddaughter occasionally. They accepted me only reluctantly, and the less I saw of them the better.

"Bye, Carl, see you tonight. Oh, honey, check to see if I turned off the coffee maker; I forgot it last week and almost ruined the pot," she called back over her shoulder.

Even after all these years the role-reversal still makes me feel foolish when I see my family off in the morning. "I will. Be careful driving in. Good-bye girls, stay out of trouble."

"Good-bye, Daddy, I love you," Julie yelled.

"I love you too, Julie."

Pam stopped at the door and looked back, saying softly, "Be careful Daddy."

I winked, and got a little smile. From the doorway I noticed Sherry pause and look down at the hood of the wagon. She glanced up and saw me watching, then moved quickly to the driver's door. As she opened it, she looked back at me and stuck out her tongue. I grinned at her as she backed out.

Fortunately, we have the kind of relationship that allows us to laugh at ourselves, as well as at each other. But it didn't start out that way. We didn't hit it off immediately. Sherry had come to work at Underhill on a Monday morning. The previous Saturday I had broken up with Mary Lou Sinclair, a very spoiled, very rich, very beautiful young blonde I dated for over three years. Actually, she broke up with me, and I wasn't happy about it at the time. So, by Monday morning I had sworn off women in general, and was, at least temporarily, immune to the smiling face and friendly chatter of the nineteen-year-old "new girl." I suppose my lack of interest showed, and Sherry reacted quite normally, deciding that I was a very rude and unpleasant fellow. It took us just under a year to go from barely acknowledging each other's presence to being hopelessly in love. We dated almost every night that first spring. On the Fourth of July, at a picnic, I asked her to marry me, and we were married the following February, on Valentine's Day. A very traditional courtship, engagement, and wedding, for a very traditional couple. Some say even boring, but what the hell, it works, and that's all that matters.

The big old house seems awfully empty when I'm by myself. I grew up here, with two older sisters. They both married and moved away while I was still in high school, one to Maine, the other to California. After our parents died, I let my sisters split the savings account, and they let me have title to the house. What we didn't need to spend on rent or house payments went into upkeep.

It's a relatively old house for this part of the country, built in the early 1900s. The original owner was Howard Clay, a rancher who appreciated the finer things in life. He started out with several square miles of grazing land, and raised cattle and horses until oil was discovered on his property. After that the abundance of riches went to his head, as did the immense quantity of imported wines and whiskeys of which he was so fond. He gradually sold off the land, until when he died in 1930, the house stood on only a half-acre lot, surrounded by smaller farms. By the time my parents bought it in 1939, the house had all the modern conveniences, including indoor plumbing. It was fully electric, though many of the original oil lamps and chandeliers are still in place.

With two stories, a basement, an attic, twelve rooms, and two fireplaces, it had only one bathroom until after Julie was born. We decided if we were going to raise two daughters in that house, we would need another bathroom. I started the renovation myself, spent two months tearing up the place, and finally had a contractor come in and do it right. After that Sherry was careful about what she asked me to do around the house.

My dad had been a shrewd banker, a wise investor, and an astute advisor to State politicians for many years. A mover and shaker, as they say, though one who preferred to stay in the background, avoiding public notice wherever possible. His name appeared in the news regularly, though seldom his picture, and when it came to his business and political activities, rumors greatly outnumbered known facts. To the world at large he was an unknown quantity. To me, he was a warm, friendly giant who used to take me for long walks along a nearby creek, who taught me how to hunt and fish, and talked to me for hours about things I didn't really understand but which nevertheless held my attention; and whose large rough hands were skilled at carving little animals out of bars of soap. My sisters were a little afraid of him, I think, or I suppose awed would better describe their feelings. He traveled a lot, and the girls never seemed to spend much time with him even when he was at home. He loved them, deeply, but he was big, and gruff, and they just never grew as close to him as I did. My mother was, perhaps, intimidated by him, even though they were very much in love. But for me, he was . . . well, he was my dad. He died when I was twenty-three years old, one month to the day after my mother had succumbed to pneumonia. They left a void in the world, as well as in me.

I finished dressing, poured a third cup of coffee, and went to my office, an eight-by-ten room off the kitchen that used to be a pantry. It's furnished with a desk, filing cabinets, typewriter, phone, and a small safe. The one window looks out onto the fenced back yard where I fought Indians and hunted grizzly bear as a boy, and where I can now watch my daughters as they serve imaginary tea to imaginary friends.

I started my workday by pulling out the Jennings file and reviewing everything I had done to date. It was a simple case and I had spent most of my time interviewing Norma Jennings' friends. They were a mixed lot, some with wealthy parents and some from the streets. They had all been willing to discuss Norma and her new boyfriend, but nothing they said helped. Everyone agreed that she and "Peppermint" had probably set up housekeeping somewhere, but ideas of where ranged from East Harlem to Miami.

Midmorning I remembered to call my answering service.

"Hello, Connie? This is Carl Jacobs. Any messages for me?"

"Yes Mr. Jacobs, we have two," Connie informed me. "Mr. Kellogg, with Underhill Insurance called at 9:00 A.M. this morning. He wants you to stop by today and see him, if you have time. Mr. Jennings, at Interstate Bank and Trust, telephoned at 9:13 A.M. He wants you to call him back right away. He said he's at the office."

"Okay Connie, thanks." I dialed Jennings' office, wondering if he had information which would help me understand why this case had almost cost me my life.

"Jacobs, I should have let you know Friday, but we were so delighted, it simply slipped my mind. Norma telephoned us Friday morning, from Tampa Bay. Her . . . friend had tried to transact some business there, and was arrested. She was stranded, broke, and wanted to come home. Her mother and I flew down, picked her up and brought her back. It's all over now. If you'll send me a bill for your services, I'll forward a check. Please include whatever time you spent this weekend. You couldn't have known she had returned."

"Well, I'm glad everything worked out for you, Mr. Jennings. I'll mail my report today. By the way, did your daughter ever mention what her friend's real name was?"

"No. Does it matter now?" he asked. "We'd like to forget about all of this, and get our lives back to normal."

"No, Sir, I don't suppose it matters. I was just curious. Let me know if you ever need anything else."

"I will, thank you. Good-bye."

"Good-bye." I knew damn well his home life would never again be what he wanted it to be. However, my concern now was to forget about the Jennings girl and start trying to figure out who wanted me dead. If I ruled out the Jennings case, I was left with an empty desk. The last two cases I had worked were for Underhill Insurance, strictly routine. Reports had been filed, and I received checks for both of them. I decided to hell with it, finished the Jennings report, typed up an invoice, and then got ready to drop in at Underhill to pick up whatever new cases they had for me.

I never know where my cases might take me, though for the most part I work the Tulsa area. That takes in a lot of territory. Tulsa has grown outward, gradually consuming or abutting several surrounding communities. Boxing the compass, to the north lie Turley and Sperry, then Skiatook; to the northeast, Owasso and Collinsville; to the east and a little south, Broken Arrow, the largest of all the nearby communities. Southeast lies Bixby, about fourteen miles away on highway 64. To the southwest is Jenks, a small community made up primarily of antique shops; and a little further along, on highway 75, is Glenpool; to the west lies Sand Springs. All of these towns have their own city police, utilities, and educational systems, yet in some cases it is hard to tell where Tulsa leaves off and where the next town begins.

Incorporated within Tulsa itself are several areas which seem to have a small-town feeling of their own, such as Brookside, Dawson (which used to be a town all by itself), Greenwood, and West Tulsa. Any way you slice it, Tulsa is large and diverse, not exactly your typical plains-state city. Even with the population approaching 350,000, it's still managed to retain some of the "small town" feel. Tulsa started out small, in 1907, but as a result of the oil boom, quickly grew into a major metropolis, with a large, international airport that at one time had more traffic each day than any other airport in the country. Now Tulsa's on a waterway to the Gulf of Mexico, providing inexpensive transportation of goods to deep water ports.

We have the standard proportionate mixture of Black, Hispanic, Oriental, and assorted European races which might occur in any coastal city, but on a smaller scale. Tulsa has more than its share of traffic, since much of the population is reasonably affluent, and families normally average two or three cars each. Drugs were around even back when I was in high school, but in the last ten or fifteen years the problem has escalated. Tulsa is geographically situated on major routes for both east-west and north-south interstate traffic—drug traffic as well as fruits and vegetables.

Many people who are simply passing through Tulsa find it so pleasant they decide to come back and stay permanently. Unfortunately, not all of them are the kind of newcomers we are looking for. So here in the quiet Bible-belt we too find ourselves hip-pocket deep in drugs, prostitution, gambling, assorted gangs, and violence. Also quite a lot of insurance fraud. That's my specialty.

The unpredictable October weather had started the day with clear skies, but the temperature was low enough to make my old corduroy sport coat appropriate, worn with a brown tie, yellow shirt, and brown slacks. My overcoat was ruined, but I dug out an old trench coat. Before leaving, I opened the ancient safe in the office and selected a Smith & Wesson Airweight Bodyguard to slip into my coat pocket. It's a funny-looking little revolver—it only holds five rounds—but the shrouded hammer and light weight make it an ideal pocket gun.

Lying on the shelf with the revolver was an assortment of switchblades. I hesitated, debating, then picked one—a slender, black, beautifully ugly automatic knife made in Taiwan. The metal handle warmed in my hand. As I pressed the button forward, a black three-inch blade appeared as if by magic, thrust through an opening at the end of the handle. Pull the button back, and the blade disappears, safely tucked away.

The feel and weight of the knife in my hand brought back schoolboy memories of friends and enemies, dark alleys and the smell of stale beer. I remembered when Jimmy and I. . . .

I had to take a cab back to the scene of the shooting to pick up my van. I found it safe and sound, right where I left it Saturday night. Even the hungriest car thief would most likely pass it by. On the outside it's a dirty gray 1976 Chevy Cargo Van. The tires are brand new but I've used brown paint to make them look old and worn to match the rest of the vehicle. The engine has been rebuilt, tuned to perfection, and the sad-looking old van will go as fast as I would ever care to drive.

Inside, the van is fully equipped for surveillance operations, with a 35mm single-lens reflex carrying a telephoto lens, a video camera, a shotgun microphone, tape recorders, a cell phone, police band scanner, an ice chest, and several plastic water bottles, both full and empty. The small windows I had installed in each side, as well as the ones in the rear cargo doors, are heavily tinted to conceal me from passing pedestrians. The wooden ladder strapped to the top gives the surveillance vehicle a rather generic work-vehicle appearance, and it blends right in almost anywhere.

Before driving away, I took a masochistic look inside the alley. I didn't expect to find anything, and I didn't. Maybe I wanted to tell Jimmy good-bye. Maybe I wanted to tell him to go to hell for complicating my life. Or maybe I just wanted to tell him I was sorry.

Another nice thing about the van is that even in downtown Tulsa I can get away with parking in one of the many loading zones near 3rd Street and Boston Avenue, as I do when calling at Underhill Insurance Company. Leaving the elevator at the 18th floor, I turned left and almost bumped into Andy Baker, one of the adjusters that worked with Sherry. His expensive gray suit was meant to hide the paunch but it didn't quite make it. The sunlamp tan would look phony even in July. He and Sherry didn't get along, and I suppose her opinion of him had influenced me, but I didn't like him much either.

"Hello, Andy. How's the insurance business?" He looked a little put out at being delayed, but he forced a smile.

"About the same, I guess. How's our very own super cop? Catching all the bad guys and making the city safe for big business?" He was careful to hide the sneer.

"It's a living. As long as your agents keep selling big money policies to the accident-prone, I guess I'll get by."

"Fortunately, Jacobs, they're not my agents. They're someone else's responsibility." He used the palm of one hand to smooth the thinning strands of hair back over a slightly red scalp. "If you're looking for Sherry, she's out examining what's left of a shoe store that burned to the ground last night. The owner was on our doorstep this morning, waiting to file a two-million-dollar claim. Stick around. Kellogg may want you to go out and sift ashes."

He stepped around me and disappeared down the hallway toward the large bull-pen room he shares with Sherry and one other adjuster. I continued in the other direction, and after a brief wait was admitted to the equally large, though more comfortably furnished office of J. W. Kellogg, the white-haired, nearsighted bulldog who runs Underhill Insurance: the only man I've ever met who could lead and drive people at the same time.

"Jacobs, I'm glad you could make it so soon. I have two files here on claims I want investigated. I won't take the time to go into details now, but they're both bodily injury claims, both high-dollar, and I want you to initiate surveillance on both of them as soon as possible. I'm tired of paying out hundreds of thousands of dollars to people who think all they need to do is complain about a sore back, and live off us for the rest of their lives. Everything you need to know should be in the files. If you have any questions, check with Andy Baker; he's the adjuster. Send me copies of the video when you're through." He handed me the folders and opened another file on his desk. I was about to leave when he stopped me. "I read about the shooting. Nothing to do with us, I suppose?"

"No, Sir. Not as far as I know. I still don't know why he did it."

"You knew him, I understand."

"Yessir."

"Just shows you, I guess. Friendships don't always last."

"No, I guess not."

He dropped his gaze back to the file on his desk, muttering, "Glad you came out of it all right." He shuffled through some papers, apparently having forgotten all about me. I was dismissed.

Clouds were gathering overhead as I hurried back to the van, wondering how I was going to handle two surveillances simultaneously. As I slipped the key into the door lock, the window shattered in front of my nose. I thought, How the hell could sticking a key in the lock break the window? Then I noticed the small round hole in the upper left corner and realized I had been shot at.

CHAPTER FOUR

Passing faces reflected first puzzlement, then fright, as I ran around to the curb side, hugging the van, digging for the .38 in my coat pocket. I swiveled my head frantically from side to side, trying to look everywhere at once. When I was certain there would be no more shots, I climbed into the van and sped away, my palms sweaty on the steering wheel. Whoever wanted me dead had found a professional. One who used a silencer.

I stopped just around the corner, out of range, and tried to call a cop, but my cell phone battery was dead. I drove to the police station, less than six blocks away, and reported the shooting in person. The officer I spoke with, Detective Sergeant Gilley, was a pompous, lazy little prick who was busy trying to keep his cigar lit and didn't have time to listen to wild stories about broken windows. He decided the shot was probably the result of kids messing around, maybe a ricochet from a distance, which would account for no one hearing anything. He was a little more interested after I explained that I was the guy who had been shot at two days earlier, and as a result had killed a man in self-defense. He said he thought he remembered reading something about it in the paper.

We found a few pieces of the slug stuck in the headliner above the windshield, enough to determine that it was probably .22 caliber, but not enough to send to ballistics for a match. Gilley called Detective Sergeant Samuel Fry, who had interrogated me Saturday night. After he hung up, Gilley told me that Detective Fry had suggested that I stop in to see him before I left. Fry's office was down the hall, near the stairs. He had also mentioned that I could pick up my automatic at the property room while I was there. Under the circumstances I thought that was a good idea.

Detective Fry greeted me on a friendlier note than at our last meeting. "Come on back, Mr. Jacobs. Sit right there. Would you care for a cup of coffee?"

"No thanks, not right now."

"Tell me about this latest shooting."

I went over it again, trying to stress the point that a silencer had been used, which indicated to me that it was a professional attempt.

"Mr. Jacobs, have you come up with a name, or even a reason why someone would want you dead?"

"I don't know any more than I did Saturday. I can't think of anyone who would have reason to kill me, unless it's someone from the past, maybe someone I worked a case on. A fraud or possibly an arson. Most of my cases are insurance-related. The only other things I handle on a regular basis would be missing persons, such as lost relatives or runaways. I haven't worked a criminal case in a couple of years. I might have cost someone a lot of money when their claim was denied, but it's very rare for criminal charges to be filed in insurance fraud. If no charges were filed, no one went to jail, and if they didn't go to jail, why wait till now to take a shot at me?"

"You say there is nothing you're working on now that might account for these attacks? I think you mentioned Saturday something about a pusher named Peppermint?"

"I was called off that case this morning. Peppermint is now in a Tampa jail, has been since Friday, and the Jennings girl is safe at home."

"Any marital problems?"

I wasn't insulted by the question, though I knew Sherry would have been. I knew most murders, aside from drug-related shootings, involved married couples having a little spat. I kept my answer simple. "No."

Fry leaned back in his chair, arms crossed over his chest, frowning at the top of his desk. After a moment's consideration, he looked up at me, questioningly. "Mr. Jacobs, are you acquainted with a private investigator by the name of Philip Foster?"

"I was. He was found dead in Broken Arrow last . . ." It took a few seconds, but I finally got it. "Are you thinking there might be some connection?"

"Not really, but a few people have mentioned the possibility. How well did you know Mr. Foster?"

"Not very well at all. We ran into each other occasionally, but we never worked together. I didn't think much of him, to tell the truth."

"The two of you never worked for the same client, or on the same investigation?"

"No, not that I know of. We might have had the same client, but it would have been on separate occasions. We both have insurance companies and law firms for clients, and clients do change investigators once in a while."

He wasn't paying attention anymore. He was looking back over my shoulder toward the door. As he stood up, I did too. When I turned around, I was face to face with the meanest-looking human I had ever seen. I managed not to take a step back, but just barely.

"Mr. Jacobs, I want you to meet a friend of mine, Detective Sergeant Albert Sweet. Detective Sweet is with the Broken Arrow Police Department. He's handling the Foster investigation. I asked him to meet us here to talk things over. Al, this is Mr. Carl Jacobs, the Private Investigator I told you about."

I've met enough cops to know they don't like to shake hands with people they meet professionally, so I didn't offer my hand first, but when Detective Sweet stuck out his, I did likewise. My extra large hand disappeared inside his fist. I expected to hear bones crush, but his grip was surprisingly gentle. His voice was more in keeping with his appearance, sounding like a rock slide. "Pleased to meet you, Mr. Jacobs. Sit down, sit down. Thanks for calling me, Fry. I could use a little hint on this one."

As I watched Sweet pull up a metal folding chair from a nearby table, I tried to decide exactly what made him so frightening. He was big, but not any taller than I was. He probably weighed over three hundred pounds, and that made him intimidating, but it finally occurred to me that his upper lip was permanently arced at one side, giving him a perpetual sneer, while his jutting forehead and dark bushy eyebrows gave the effect of two eyes peering forth from the depths of a cave. He was square. All over. His head, nose, chin, shoulders, hands—everything was square, with no softness showing anywhere.

"Mr. Jacobs, Fry tells me you were attacked in an alley Saturday night. He says you had to kill a man by the name of Jimmy Jay, but you can't explain why this Jay would want to kill you, and that you and he went to school together. Now I understand you were shot at again this morning, and you still don't know why. We might be able to keep you alive if you could come up with a motive for someone to want you dead."

"Believe me, I'm more interested than you are in finding out what this is all about, but so far there isn't any reason at all that I can think of. Do you really think my troubles are tied in with Foster getting shot?"

"Were you two working together on anything?"

"No, I explained to Detective Fry that I knew Foster, casually, but we never worked together. We may have worked for the same people somewhere along the way, but if we did I don't know about it."

"We've put together a list of clients out of his files, and we'd like to compare it with your cases, if that's okay with you," Sweet requested.

"Sure, no problem. Do you want me to make a list, with dates, or would you rather go through the files yourself? I don't guess I have to mention that the files are confidential. To protect my credibility with my clients, I think it would be best for you to get a warrant for the files, instead of me handing them over to you."

"That's probably not necessary at this point, Mr. Jacobs. Put together a list of clients and the dates. If we get a match that looks promising, then we'll worry about the subject of the investigation, and the details."

"You don't think there's some nut running around trying to kill off private investigators, do you? We make a few enemies once in a while. Maybe someone snapped." It didn't sound right to me, even as I said it.

"In this city anything's possible. We'll have to look into it a little more before we know anything for sure. In the meantime, you may solve the problem for us if the guy tries again. You didn't have much trouble with the Blue Jay."

"Jimmy wasn't a gunman, Detective Sweet. Whoever is doing the shooting now is using a silenced .22, which probably means an experienced killer. I'm not sure it's all tied together, anyway. Maybe this shooting today was an accident, like Gilley said. Maybe Foster was killed by some punk trying to steal his watch," I said, without much conviction.

Friends and Other Perishables

Fry nodded his head. "That's what I think. I don't see any connection. You guys want a cup of coffee?" We declined, and he left to fill his own cup.

When he was far enough away not to hear, Sweet, speaking in a low rumbling voice, said, "I'm afraid there is a connection, Mr. Jacobs, but I would appreciate you keeping this to yourself for now. After I heard about your shooting Saturday night, I requested a copy of the ballistics report. The .38 Special Jimmy Jay used on you was the same weapon that killed Foster two weeks ago."

I had to think that over for a minute, then against my better judgment inquired, "Why don't you want Fry to know?"

"It's my case, damnit! Foster was shot in Broken Arrow. Fry will know soon enough, but for now it gives me an edge, and God knows I need it," he growled.

"What the hell, are you guys in some sort of competition? I thought you were all on the same team. If you'll forgive the expression."

He swallowed his first contemplated remark then said patiently, "It's not between me and Fry. It's . . . I . . . you see, I'm in a little trouble with my Chief. A while back I made an arrest. A john beat up a hooker, one of my snitches. I picked him up, and in the process of making the arrest . . . well, he resisted a little, and I had to persuade him to come quietly. Peacefully. Actually, he was unconscious by the time we reached the station, and . . . Well, it turns out he's married to a friend of a relative of . . . Hell. You know how it works. I got an ass chewing and a warning. I need to break this case to take some of the pressure off. Okay?"

"Okay by me," I agreed, hoping he never had occasion to persuade me to come quietly.

Sweet continued, "It looks like your friend Jay was more experienced than you give him credit for. He killed Foster, then he tried to take you out. They found ninety-five hundred dollars in cash in Jay's apartment, and he had three hundred dollars on him when he died. If Foster was worth ten thousand dollars, you probably are too. All we have to do now is find out who paid Jay to pull the trigger, why, and who's out there now trying to finish the job." He stood up and moved to the door, waving good-bye to Fry.

Sure. That's all we have to do.

CHAPTER FIVE

Before leaving the police station I stopped by the property room, showed them the release Detective Fry had signed, and picked up my .45 Colt Automatic. It's the Lightweight Commander, and I feel about it the way Linus does about his baby blanket. Before I went home I dropped the van off at Metro Auto Glass, making arrangements to have the window replaced. They said I could pick it up the next day. I thought it was polite of them not to question me about the obvious bullet hole. They even called a taxi to take me home.

Back at the house I spent an hour cleaning and oiling the automatic. I wanted to make sure it was in good condition, just in case I might need it again, soon. After that, I went through my files covering the last three months, making a list of clients' names, dates, and the type of investigation: whether it was an arson, bodily injury, witness locate, a surveillance, or whatever. It took me the rest of the afternoon because I read each case thoroughly, trying to find something that might be linked to the attempts on my life. They all seemed pretty trivial when looked at in that light. When I had finished, I felt I had lost ground. I was more confused than when I started.

By the time Sherry and the girls came home I had put together a dinner of biscuits, grilled pork chops, mashed potatoes and gravy, carrots, and a green salad to pacify my health-conscious wife. Pam and Julie were unusually quiet. It turned out they both had upcoming tests, so after they helped their mother with the dishes, they spent the evening in their room, studying. Sherry and I curled up in front of the fireplace. She talked about her day at the office, occasionally pausing to slap my hands and remind me the girls may pop in at any moment.

"Damn it, Carl, stop it."

"Okay."

"What are you doing way over there?"

"You said to stop it. I've stopped."

"I didn't say go hide. Come back here."

"Okay."

"Damnit, Carl! Whoo! Stop it."

We eventually worked out a compromise, which didn't really satisfy either of us, but it was still early.

"Carl?"

"Hmmm?"

"Do you want to talk about Jimmy?"

"Not especially. Do you?"

"Well, I think it's terrible, that he would try to . . . hurt you. Are you sure he knew what he was doing?"

"What, you think I killed him by accident?"

"No. Of course not. You know what I mean. You two were friends, you've known each other for years. Why would he all of a sudden try to shoot you? Carl, he's been to our house. He met the girls, brought them birthday presents. I don't understand how he could turn around and do such a thing."

She buried her face under my chin, her forehead pressed against my neck. I could feel her breath, soft and warm. I didn't want to think about old friends, and death. I didn't have any answers. "I don't think he would have, on his own. I think he was probably hired by someone. Or maybe he was forced by someone into doing what he did. I'd like to think it wasn't an easy thing for him to do."

I could feel Sherry suddenly stiffen in my arms. She slowly pulled away, sat up, and looked at me with something like dread in her eyes.

"He was broke, wasn't he? You think he needed money for something? Was he desperate, Carl? Oh my God!" She covered her face with both hands.

"Sherry? What is it? What's wrong?"

"It was my fault. I wouldn't let him have the money. Don't you see? It was my fault."

"What the hell are you talking about? What money?"

"Jimmy's claim. I told you about it. Didn't I?"

"This is the first I've heard about any claim. Jimmy filed an insurance claim? With Underhill?"

"Yes. Carl, I thought I had . . . I guess I forgot. It was two or three months ago. I ran across a claims form with Jimmy's name on it. It was absolutely ridiculous. He was filing a burglary claim, on a policy he only took out two months before. His claim showed a loss of over eighteen thousand dollars. It was for jewelry, appliances, even a couple of antique vases. I knew damn well Jimmy never had any of those things. I called his landlord, some guy named Parker, or Parkinson, something. He said he had been inside Jimmy's apartment at least twice a month for the last year, and never saw any of the things Jimmy reported stolen. He laughed about it. Said Jimmy was always trying to come up with a scheme to make a fast buck."

"So, what did you do about it? He must have filed a phony burglary report. Did you report him to the police?"

"Of course not. He's . . . He was our friend. I wouldn't do that. But Carl, I couldn't pay that claim. You know that."

"I wouldn't expect you to. I can't believe Jimmy would expect you to pay off on it, either."

"Hell, he didn't even know I worked at Underhill. He knew I was in the insurance business, but I guess he never knew what company. When I called him and told him we were denying the claim, he fell all over himself apologizing, said it was all a mistake, and that he had been writing us a letter canceling his claim when I called. He was really surprised, and I think he was embarrassed, too. I told him to forget it, that we would drop the whole thing. Carl, he must have been desperate for money to do such a thing. And I turned him down. Don't you see? If I had paid the claim, he would have collected over eighteen thousand dollars, and no one could ever have talked him into hurting you. Carl, he might still be alive," she cried.

CHAPTER SIX

It took a couple of hours to convince Sherry she wasn't responsible for Jimmy's death. Even after a restless night she was still unusually quiet and distracted the next morning. After she and the girls were away, I put the breakfast dishes in the sink, selected a conservative blue suit, white-on-white dress shirt, and my lucky red paisley power tie from the crowded closet. Then I went to work myself.

On the surface it seems pretty stupid for a man to trot off to work in the morning when he knows someone is trying to kill him. I thought about hanging around the house for a while, trying to sort things out in my mind. Then I started wondering if I was hiding. Sometimes it's certainly a lot easier to hide, but it gets hard to live with after a while. I decided to get busy on the surveillances for Underhill. A man has to make a living. A cab took me by the repair shop to pick up the van. I took a minute to drive through a nearby car wash because the new window glass made the rest of the van look filthy.

My next stop was not far away. Obviously, even the best investigators can't work two surveillances at once. Not unless the two subjects live together. I parked at curbside in front of the little white frame house, and walked down the drive to the garage out back. I had never been in the house, but I knew the people who lived there. Mr. and Mrs. Adams were elderly, retired, and the parents of one Tal Adams, a twenty-two-year-old paraplegic, who might have gone to jail for computer "hacking" a few years ago if Underhill Insurance had decided to press charges. As it turned out, the kid's talent for breaking into large computer systems was so impressive that when word got out about him, representatives of several large corporate security departments started calling on him for tips on how to improve their own computer security systems. What started out as an interesting, though somewhat illegal, game and source of entertainment for a wheelchair-bound teenager developed into a lucrative consulting business. Maybe that was why he didn't hate me for tracking him down and spoiling the fun he was having digging around in Underhill's extensive computer files. In fact, we became pretty close friends, and I used him on almost every case. With the equipment Tal had set up in the little garage, he could research public records in every state, coast to coast, and even some foreign countries. And, he repeatedly assured me it was all legal. I repeatedly assured him, if I don't ask, I don't want to know.

The little garage was less than impressive, with paint flaking everywhere but on the painted-over windows. The new roof seemed a little out of place, but Tal figured the neighborhood petty thieves, vandals, and burglars wouldn't notice. Besides, he had a computerized intrusion alarm system that might have been designed at the Pentagon.

I didn't bother to knock on the outer door. I knew it was just the first hurdle. Only one pace inside the door, my progress was halted by a glass security door, with a badge-activated lock. The flashing red light in the ceiling eventually attracted Tal's attention and he looked up from his terminal, glanced my way, then triggered the door lock with a remote device and let me in.

"Hey, Mr. Wizard, how's it going?"

"Just fine, Carl. Where you been so long?"

"Here and there. In between, mostly."

"How about a cup of coffee? Fresh."

Friends and Other Perishables

"Sure, thanks, Tal. You got time to run a couple of names for me? No big hurry." I helped myself to the coffee from a battered Mr. Coffee pot.

"I should have them by tomorrow night, if that's okay. What do you need?"

"For now just run them through Oklahoma. Give me Criminal, Civil, Marriage, Divorce, Traffic, you know, the usual. If things get complicated we might dig deeper."

Sipping the coffee, I glanced around the room. The place looked cluttered at first, but after a second look you realized it was as neat and clean as a hospital room. It looked cluttered because it was so crowded with whirring, blinking, ticking electric . . . things.

"Damn, Tal, every time I come by here you have something new crammed into a corner, or slot, or on top of something else. What's that box over there?"

"It's an ion generator, a device that's supposed to help remove dust particles from the air. Some of this equipment tends to slow down and stop when it gets dusty. It works on smoke too, but of course I don't let anyone smoke in here."

"And that?"

"That's my new FAX. A facsimile machine. It lets me send and receive document copies, even photographs. As soon as some of my clients found out I had it, I had to buy another file cabinet to keep all the paperwork people started sending me. I'm not sure that's progress."

"What about this thing? What the hell is it?"

He paused, then, trying not to embarrass me, "An electric pencil sharpener."

When I grinned, he realized I'd probably recognized the pencil sharpener for myself, and he blushed and stammered as he always does when someone tries to kid him about something. The brown hair hanging down in his eyes, and

47

the round, wire-rimmed glasses made him look closer to sixteen than twenty-two, and I wondered, briefly, if he was going to spend the rest of his life, alone, in this tiny electric world he had built for himself.

"Well, if you have a sharpened pencil handy, you might take this down." Tal made notes as I gave him what information I had on the two surveillance subjects. "First. Mr. Dennis Holloway, male Caucasian, born 10-25-55 in Kansas City. Now lives in Brookside. Mr. Holloway was in an automobile accident in June of this year. Back and neck injury. Before the accident Mr. Holloway supposedly ran a little dry cleaners on 109th Street in Bixby. Wife and one child."

I read off Holloway's social security number and turned to the next work order. "Second. Nelson Cook, DOB 4-18-40, from Tulsa. Caucasian male, no family. He's another back injury, surprise, surprise. Slipped on a grape at his local supermarket. No witnesses. Naturally. Get me what you can on these guys, Tal. I'm going to check out their homes this morning and try to work out a surveillance plan. I'll check back with you in the morning."

"Say, Carl, before you go, could I ask a favor?"

"Sure, kid. After all the help you've been to me? Ask anything you want. What can I do for you?"

"Well, you see, I had an appointment yesterday, at Riverside Hospital. My doctor insists that I go in for periodic tests and physical therapy. For my legs. I've found it's easier to humor him than to argue. You know how doctors can be."

Tal wasn't especially touchy about the subject of his condition. We had talked about it before, and I knew he had pretty well accepted the idea that he probably would never walk again. Tal was an active, healthy kid until just after his fourteenth birthday. He was like most kids that age: already bored with life, looking for thrills, and confident in his own immortality. Tal pushed the envelope too far, however, when he tried to ride his skateboard down a concrete banister at the local civic center. At the bottom of the flight of stairs, his skateboard went one way, and he went the other, crashing to the pavement on his back. He suffered some sort of spinal injury that left him paralyzed from the waist down. At the time, almost eight years earlier, the doctors had given him no hope of ever fully recovering. Since that time, with a new medical miracle popping up every now and then, Tal's doctor had begun to talk about various treatments that may, or may not, prove beneficial. So far, nothing seemed to have helped.

"Yeah. Well, what's up? Any signs of improvement, Tal?"

"No, it's nothing like that. About all I've gotten out of it so far is a great rubdown by a young, blonde nurse's aide who still thinks computers are just expensive calculators."

"That must be worth the trip all by itself."

"Yeah, I guess so. That is, it would have been, except yesterday, while I was in X-ray, someone stole my wheelchair."

I glanced down, and for the first time I noticed he wasn't in his battery-powered chair. The chair he was in was a standard, manually operated wheelchair. A far cry from the chrome and leather Cadillac of wheelchairs he normally raced around the garage in. That wheelchair, with the little toggle steering doodad, rear-view mirror, and aahOOgha horn, had been presented to Tal two years before by the local Chamber of Commerce, in recognition for his contribution to the city's attempts to develop a virus-proof, hacker-proof, centralized data processing network for local law enforcement, city and county tax assessors, municipal utilities, and municipal libraries. The chair had a silver plaque on the back, which showed an engraved drawing of a grinning Tal, superimposed over the Tulsa city skyline, and below the picture were the words, "To Talmidge Wayne Adams, from his hometown, with much gratitude and best wishes." Tal would have given up his computer before he gave up that chair.

"What happened, Tal?"

"All I know is, when they took me into X-ray and had me lie down on that table, they pushed the wheelchair back out of the room and apparently left it out in the hallway. I was in there about ten minutes all together. When they went to get the chair, they couldn't find it. The nurse kept saying it was just moved by mistake, and they would find it soon, but after half an hour they gave me this thing as a loaner, and said they would be in touch as soon as my chair turned up. That was two o'clock yesterday afternoon. I haven't heard anything since then. I was hoping you would check it out for me, if you get a chance."

"Sure, Tal, I'd be glad to. I'll let you know if I turn up anything." I left Tal bending over his keyboard, projecting his intellect and curiosity along phone lines the length and breadth of the continent, on some adventure quest of his own. He'd get around to my problems as soon as he got bored.

An hour later I was checking out the Holloway residence in Brookside. It turned out to be a three-story walkup, and the mailbox for the Holloways was labeled 2B, which I eventually figured out meant they lived on the east side of the second floor. I had to negotiate my way around assorted pieces of garbage and empty pop cans, but I managed to

Friends and Other Perishables

walk quietly past the apartment door and heard a television playing inside, which would indicate the apartment was occupied. Of course I couldn't be sure it was Holloway until I had seen him. I knocked on the door.

The guy who opened the door matched the description I had: thirty-five years old, five feet ten inches, about one hundred eighty pounds, with brown hair and a mustache. He was wearing jeans and a coffee-stained sweatshirt. He was supposed to be wearing a neck brace and walking with a cane. He wasn't.

"Yeah?"

"Is this the Howard Carter residence?"

"Who?"

"Howard Carter. He's supposed to live here, apartment 2B, right?"

"Never heard of him." He closed the door, firmly.

Having verified the subject was at home, and having had a good look at him, I went back to my van, drove around a few minutes, eventually parking in front of a boarded up second-hand store about half a block east of the apartment building. From there, I could watch the front stoop and maybe even get a look through Holloway's windows if the lighting was just right. Since he wasn't using a cane or wearing a neck brace, at least not while at home, there was a chance I could get some good video. If he would just come outside for a while. That was what I was there for, to find out if he showed any signs of really being hurt, or if he had been strolling around the neighborhood kicking dogs and playing catch with his ten-year-old son.

Once again, as I settled down on the padded swivel seat I had installed in the rear of the van, out of sight of passing pedestrians, I wished surveillance work was a little more like the television writer's version. You know, where the handsome detective parks in front of the suspect's house in his red Ferrari convertible and waits patiently for maybe three minutes before his suspect obligingly comes out of the mansion, climbs into his black limo, and leads the dedicated detective to the scene of the next vicious crime. I suppose it would be difficult to write a popular show about long, miserable hours of cold feet, aching necks, and bursting kidneys. Television stars don't relieve themselves in plastic milk jugs, eat dry cheese sandwiches for lunch, and struggle to keep their eyes open after hours of mind-numbing boredom.

By 2:00 that afternoon I had videotaped eight different people as they entered or left the apartment building, none of them Dennis Holloway. Of the eight, only three were adult males; one tired night-shift worker apparently arriving home from the salt mines, one bill-collector/repo type, and a bug exterminator going through the motions.

At 3:20 P.M., two young boys, one Black, one Caucasian, climbed the stoop, and entered the apartment building. I figured the kids were about ten years old, and assumed the Caucasian boy was Holloway's son, Eddie, getting home from school. It occurred to me that Holloway may be coming out any minute, now that the boy was home. I got the 8mm Canon Video Camcorder ready for action, and concentrated my attention on the stoop.

At the first sign of motion near the front door, I touched the switch and started to record. It took a moment for me to understand exactly what I was seeing, and taping. Eddie Holloway was running down the steps, screaming. No one was chasing him. He ran into a small used clothing shop across the street. A moment later an elderly man came out of the store and quickly crossed the street, climbed the stoop, and disappeared inside.

Friends and Other Perishables

Needless to say, I was curious, but the first rule of working a surveillance is to stay as inconspicuous as possible, so I stayed put, out of sight inside the van. It took the ambulance about ten minutes to get there. By that time a small but growing crowd had formed at the foot of the steps leading into the shabby building. As the two attendants, one male, one female, carried the stretcher up the stoop, I felt something with cold feet walk up my spine. I knew then I would never get any videotape of Dennis Holloway playing catch with his son.

The patrol car was only a minute behind the ambulance. Less than half an hour later, an unmarked car with a couple of tired men in gray suits arrived. I recognized the shortest one as Detective Fry. Soon they were walking up and down the street, asking questions of people who had no answers. I figured, what the hell, it would come out sooner or later, so I left the van and walked over to visit with Fry and tell him I thought I had some videotape he might be interested in.

By 7:00 that evening we had unanimously agreed on only one thing. Either the man who shot Dennis Holloway in the back of the head with a silenced .22 automatic was captured on my videotape, or he wasn't.

On the pro side we had three votes for the exterminator, two votes for the tired night worker, and two votes for the bill collector. Fry, his partner, and the three patrolmen were adamant about their votes. I was still willing to go either way. We discounted the extra vote for the exterminator because it was courtesy of the station house janitor, who cast his vote while collecting our empty coffee cups and admitted he thought a murderer posing as a bug killer would make for good press.

On the other hand, it was pointed out that as a general rule sneak thieves, burglars, and murderers don't use front doors when they can avoid it, and the back entrance to the three-story apartment building where the Holloways lived was wide open and readily accessible from a deserted alley. Just like in the movies.

The six of us, not counting the janitor, had spent several hours viewing and reviewing the videotape I had obtained during my surveillance of the Holloway residence. The tape wouldn't do me or my client, Underhill Life and Casualty, a bit of good as far as Mr. Holloway's injury claim was concerned, but that was no longer an issue.

Once the police knew I had videotaped everyone going in and out of the building between the hours of 10:00 A.M. and 3:00 P.M., they, of course, thought I would be able to provide the evidence they could use to identify and arrest the killer. And I wanted him caught, certainly. Caught, convicted, drawn and quartered. After all, the son-of-a-bitch had walked right into the building and killed Holloway while I was supposed to be keeping him under surveillance. Not good for my image. Not good for my ulcer, either, and the dark thick stuff cops call coffee wasn't helping.

I was ready to call it a day. My eyes were burning from the cigarette and cigar smoke. My head hurt, probably out of anger and frustration, and my lucky red paisley power tie was folded up in the pocket of my conservative blue suit coat, which was draped over the back of the most uncomfortable metal chair I had ever sat in. I was looking around for a friendly face to advise I would gladly give them the videotape and make myself available the next day, if only they would let me go home to shower, eat, and sleep. The trouble was, there were no friendly faces in the room. Fry had been polite and patient with me, but we were all tired and tempers were getting short. I think all of them, Fry included, were thinking to themselves that things would have

Friends and Other Perishables

been a lot simpler if some nosy private dick hadn't been playing around with a video camera in front of the murder scene.

Eventually they decided they didn't need me taking up space and drinking their coffee, so I was allowed to leave. But only after I told one whopper of a lie. When Detective Fry asked me if I knew of any common denominator between Foster, the Blue Jay, my getting shot at, and my investigation of Holloway, I looked him square in the nose and said, tiredly, with great conviction, "No, Sir, not a thing that I can think of."

It was almost 9:00 P.M. when I walked through the front door, kissed Pam and Julie goodnight, and told Sherry, yes, I was hungry and would like some left-over meatloaf.

While Sherry fussed around, I sat at the little table staring at the yellow and white vertical stripes on the kitchen wallpaper. It's a warm, comfortable room. Whenever we have guests over for an evening of cards or one of the more popular word games, sooner or later everyone ends up in the kitchen, watching Sherry slice cheese and stack crackers, or ice brownies, while they take turns telling tales of in-laws, kids, geraniums, or rose bush aphids. I could have felt more comfortable than I did, but I suppose I had good cause not to.

"Rape!"

"Huh? What'd you say, Sherry?"

"I said, 'Rape,' but that was to get your attention. Talk to me. Tell me I'm silly to assume there is something terribly wrong simply because you come home in a trance. Tell me you're tired, or tell me you're trying to decide what to get me for my birthday. You can tell me almost anything. I definitely do not want you to tell me you had to kill someone else, and for God's sake, don't tell me someone is still trying to kill you."

I pushed my chair back from the table and pulled her down to sit on my lap. Her small hands pressed tightly against my back. She hid her face against my neck, afraid of what I might say, more afraid of not knowing.

"I was working a surveillance today. For Underhill. A man named Holloway sustained a back injury in an auto accident. Your boss thinks it's a questionable claim, and he asked me to get video of the guy. No big deal. Same old stuff, right?"

"Right. Now tell me what turns it into a big deal. What's the new stuff?"

"While I was sitting in Brookside, waiting for him to come out of his apartment building and turn cartwheels down the sidewalk so I could take his picture, someone fired two slugs from a .22 automatic into the back of Holloway's skull. Now, you tell me it's just a coincidence, and that I'd be wasting my time trying to make more than that out of it."

She got up from my lap, staring into my eyes as she backed away, moved around the table and sat across from me. "Carl, what the hell is going on? That's . . . what? Two dead men, and two times you've been shot at in just a few days? That doesn't make sense. You've been doing this for years, and nothing like this has ever happened before. Why now?"

"Three dead men, actually."

"Three?"

"The police have proof that Foster's death is connected somehow. At least some of them do. I fortunately forgot to mention that Jimmy's gun was used to kill Foster before I left the boys in blue. And gray. If I had brought all that into it, they'd still have me down there answering questions when your birthday rolls around, and I wouldn't have to worry about what to get you. Besides, Sweet asked me to keep it to myself, and Sweet's the kind of cop you like to keep happy."

She puzzled that over for a minute as she removed a slab of meatloaf from the microwave and placed it on a plate next to a pile of green beans and a slice of garlic toast. She set the plate in front of me, added a glass of iced tea from a pitcher in the refrigerator, and sat back down across from me, deep in thought. She didn't notice when I got up and walked across the room to get a knife and fork from the silverware drawer. And she never spoke, as I slowly finished my impromptu meal. She's a good wife.

Before we turned in for the night I made a call and determined Detective Albert Sweet was still available. I'm not sure why I chose to work with him instead of any one of the other officers I had spoken with during the last few days. Perhaps simply because his sheer size and physical appearance had made a lasting impression on me. Or maybe it was because he was working the Foster homicide, and that was where all this mess started. In any event, I caught him at his desk, even though it was after 10:00 P.M.

"Detective Sweet, this is Carl Jacobs. Sorry to bother you so late, but I think you should know about something that happened this afternoon."

I laid it out for him, how a claimant I had under surveillance was murdered with a .22 automatic pistol, probably with a silencer. The same type of weapon someone had tried to use on me. His questions showed he was thinking along the same line I was.

"Anything to tie Holloway to the Blue Jay, or Foster?"

"Not that I know of so far, but right now I'd have to bet money that we'll find something eventually. Believe me, my life up to now has included damn few shootings. I've got a man running a background check on Holloway, but I won't have the results until tomorrow night."

"I imagine we can handle that. Who's working the Holloway investigation?"

"Detective Fry and his partner. I didn't get his name. Sweet, I didn't tell them about Jimmy's gun being used on Foster. That's going to leave me way out on a limb. If this all comes back on me, I'm going to need you to help me explain."

"Holloway being shot could be a coincidence. Stranger things have happened."

I didn't even try to respond to that. I knew damn well he wasn't even considering the possibility of coincidence. There was a long pause on the other end. Eventually I heard him take a deep breath. "I'll take care of it. I'll want to see you tomorrow, Jacobs."

I assured him he could reach me at home if he called early enough. He suggested I wait to hear from him till hell froze over if necessary. I agreed, meekly, and gave him my phone number. I said goodnight, but all I got back was a dial tone.

By the time I had showered, Sherry was already in bed. I tried not to disturb her as I slid under the covers, but she was still awake. We lay quietly, her head on my chest. She has an uncanny sense for knowing when I need to talk, and when I would rather not. We were both deep in thought, working on the same puzzle, looking at the same pieces from different angles. We were warm and safe in each other's arms. But we didn't sleep well.

CHAPTER SEVEN

Once upon a time, long, long ago when I was sixteen years old, there was another night when I couldn't get to sleep. After churning the bed covers for over an hour I got up, slipped on my robe, and went downstairs to the kitchen. I had taken the first bite out of a ham and cheese sandwich when my father walked into the kitchen, also in his robe. They were matching robes, presents from Mom. She did things like that.

"What's wrong? Are you in trouble again?" He never was one to edge his way into a conversation. He poured us both a glass of milk while he waited for my answer.

"No, Dad. What makes you think I'm in any trouble?"

"I'm your father, I know when something's bothering you. You didn't eat your dinner, and now I find you in the kitchen with a sandwich at midnight." He paused, looking at me carefully. "Does it have anything to do with those bruises on your jaw and neck you've been trying to hide all evening?"

After considering several different answers, I decided to get it over with. "Yeah, I guess it does."

"I take it you didn't win."

"No, Sir. I didn't."

"No excuses? You're not going to tell me he was bigger than you, or that there were three or four, or ten of them?"

"No. I don't have an excuse. He was just tougher than me, that's all."

Another long pause, then, "Were you in the right?"

"Yes, Sir. I think I was."

"Well, son, it's a hard lesson, but contrary to what the cowboy movies teach, right doesn't always win out. Sometimes the bad guys come out on top. At least, temporarily."

We both sat and thought about that for a moment. Then, as usual, he put his finger directly on the problem. "So, what are you going to do about it?"

"I really don't know, Sir." I remembered a time four years earlier when Jimmy and I had been assaulted by two drunks in an alley. Jimmy got away from them, but they grabbed me. I had managed to wound both of them with a switchblade knife, something I shouldn't have had in the first place, but which damn sure came in handy on that occasion, and while they were screaming and cursing me, I ran home and went straight to my room after apologizing to my mother for being late returning from a trip to the movies with my friend Jimmy. I never told Mom or Dad what had happened. For days I expected the police to show up at the house and arrest me, possibly for murder. I didn't know whether the two men had lived or bled to death in the alley. I swore Jimmy to secrecy, threatening him with dire consequences if he ever told a soul. After washing the knife in kerosene to remove all blood and fingerprints, I had wrapped it in plastic and buried it in the back yard. I was wondering if the knife was still there, and whether I should dig it up and start carrying it again. It used to provide me with a sense of security I no longer had.

Dad broke into my thoughts, remarking, "Well, I might have an idea. We'll see."

The next morning, Saturday, a day I will always remember, my Dad surprised me with an invitation to have lunch with him at a Denny's restaurant. While we were waiting for our order, a dark, stocky man approached our booth. I was really surprised when Dad quickly rose, and shook hands with the newcomer, saying, "Good afternoon, Sir. Thank you for coming."

I had never heard my father call anyone "Sir" before. I looked at this man closely, as he slid into the booth next to my father, who nodded toward me and said, "This is my son, Carl. Carl, I would like for you to meet Roger Graye. I have asked him to accept you as a student."

The man held out his hand to me, and I took it. He seemed young, at first, then upon closer scrutiny, I could see tiny wrinkles around the eyes which might have indicated he was much older. His grasp was as gentle as his voice when he spoke. "How do you do, Carl? I'm happy to meet you. You wish to become my student, like your father?"

My father, a student? Of what?

"Like I used to be, anyway. Mr. Graye operates a Karate Dojo, Carl. A school. He is going to teach you how to handle yourself," my father explained.

"Karate?" I almost laughed. Big mistake. "I thought that was just . . . uh . . . well, I mean . . ."

"You thought karate was just for the movies, right?" Mr. Graye smiled as he explained to me that karate was very real indeed, and very effective. My father was not smiling. Mr. Graye turned to him. "He is a little old to be starting now."

"Yes, he's sixteen. But I was twenty-four when I started," my father replied, to my amazement. I thought I knew my father as well as anyone, but I was beginning to think otherwise.

After studying me closely Mr. Graye again turned to my father. "Tell me, William, why do you not teach Carl yourself? You are certainly qualified."

My father glanced quickly at me before answering, and I thought he sounded almost embarrassed, as he admitted, "I may not be able to apply the discipline necessary to obtain the best results. He is my son, and I might fail in my duty as his teacher because of my affection for him. To teach him only a part of the whole would do more harm than good."

"Very well. Carl, if you will accept me as your instructor, I will welcome you as my student. I have known your father for many years. If you are as good a student as he, you will honor me, as he has done. When do you want to start?"

"Uh . . . well, Sir, I don't know."

"He will start today," my father said. And I did.

There followed three years of training, two nights each week, and two hours on Saturdays. Mr. Graye would not allow his school-age students to train any more than that. He demanded that we direct our efforts as much toward our education as to our training. But while he had us there, he was relentless, demanding ever more from our young, growing bodies.

I began in a class with children, much to my embarrassment. The oldest was twelve, a slender, quiet boy with blonde hair, glasses, and a shy smile. He was three inches shorter than me, and he got my attention during the first class when he repeatedly managed to throw me to the mat, with seemingly little effort. By the end of that first session I was determined to become proficient at karate.

Mr. Graye, who would not allow us to address him as Sensi, or Teacher, trained us in a Korean style karate, similar to Kenpo. He focused on basic movements, blocks, punches, and throws, for the entire first year of training. We were warned to seek perfection, not promotion, and only the lower rank belts, white, orange, purple, and green, could be earned during the first two years of training. The coveted brown and black belts seemed forever beyond our grasp, while students in other disciplines throughout the city were earning their black belts in less than a year. In spite of his strictness, and his failure to bribe us with colored belts of ever increasing rank, I respected him, admired him, and grew to love him, as I had no other man, save my father.

I recall one evening, when I was not scheduled for a training session, I visited the school to purchase a new gi, as my old uniform had grown too tight around the chest. As I stood in the front office area I heard a class in progress. A small waiting room off to one side was equipped with a few chairs and provided a window through which anxious parents, who brought their children to class, could watch the proceedings unobtrusively.

The waiting room was empty, but when I looked through the window, what I saw both thrilled and encouraged me. The class consisted of ten men and women, of all ages, wearing brown belts. They were being put through their paces by two men and one woman, all of whom wore the prized black belt. Mr. Graye stood to one side and supervised. I watched in awe as these men and women went through their forms and sparring sessions with a precision I had previously thought impossible. They were performing, primarily, the same movements, blocks and punches, kicks and throws, that I and my classmates were learning in our basic class, but the level of performance was so much greater that it had the appearance of an entirely different discipline.

Even at this level, there were none of the flying, spinning, jumping maneuvers that we saw so often at tournaments, performed by students of other disciplines. We were taught to use linear punching with circular blocks and to advance or retreat, as the occasion dictated, in a direct line or on the oblique. Kicks were seldom directed higher than the belt, and our sparring techniques were almost entirely drawn from the kata, or forms, that we performed for exercise and training—though the kata movements were not always recognized as such, when put to actual use in a sparring match.

The formula drilled into us, over and over, was first, avoid conflict if at all possible; second, if conflict was inevitable, it should be brought to an end as quickly as possible; third, the primary goal is to block your opponent's attack, disable your opponent with accurate, controlled blows, and when your opponent is down or disabled, leave the area. We were also taught that while spinning back kicks and jump kicks are pretty to watch and effective in a ring when combatants are wearing karate gi's and are bare-footed, such techniques are extremely risky when wearing street clothes, shoes, and fighting on concrete surfaces. A better approach under those circumstances is to keep both feet on the ground, maintain balance and total control over your body, and end the conflict with as little energy as might be required to get the job done.

I do not know how long I stood there, open-mouthed, watching. I only know that when I managed to tear myself away, before anyone knew I was there, I left the school more determined than ever to continue my training until I could perform up to that standard.

Three years later, after a great deal of sweat, pain, and effort, I believed I had slowly but surely arrived at a level of performance to qualify for my brown belt. I was excited and pleased when Mr. Graye invited me to attend an evening session with his brown belt class. I was to be tested for my promotion to that ranking before a board made up of Mr. Graye, his three black belt students, and another instructor visiting from Oklahoma City. The test was to be Tuesday

"Well, he's going about it the right way." I crossed to the door, peered through the spy hole, and then, after assuring the girls everything was okay, I opened the door and admitted Detective Albert Sweet.

Sweet had about the same effect on Sherry and the girls that he had on me the first time I saw him. For a moment I thought he was unaware of their apprehension, which didn't seem likely, and then I thought I caught a faint twinkle in his eye as he solemnly rumbled his "Good morning."

As I introduced him, I watched Sherry without surprise as she calmly looked Sweet up and down, taking his measure while her hand rested in his, and apparently arrived at the conclusion that Sweet was a man to be trusted. Possibly even respected and admired. She communicated her approval to me with a glance, and then introduced the girls by name, nodding her reassurance as they timidly held out their hands. The girls accepted their mother's verdict, as we all were inclined to do, though I could almost hear their sighs of relief as they drew back all five fingers.

"Detective Sweet, how do you drink your coffee?"

"Uh, black, Ma'am. But please don't bother."

"It's no bother, the coffee's already made. I'm sure you and Carl have a lot to talk about. If you'll make yourself comfortable, there'll be coffee and rolls in a minute. Or would you prefer toast?"

"No Ma'am, a roll will be fine, thank you."

Sherry disappeared toward the kitchen, closely followed by Pam and Julie. I pointed Sweet to my favorite chair, and sat on the couch to his left after moving an assortment of school books to one side.

"Nice family."

"Thanks. Are you married?"

"Yeah. I've got five boys. No girls, yet. My wife still

evening. That morning, Mr. Graye was crossing the s
in front of the school when he was struck by a pickup tı
driven by a drunk driver. Mr. Graye was pronounced d
at the scene. My dad and I attended Mr. Graye's funeral
gether. That was the one and only time I ever saw him cı
He had seen me cry before.

A year later, while attending Tulsa University, majoring
in political science, I discovered combat pistol competition.
One of my classmates was named in the local newspaper as
having won a regional championship, and I asked him about
it. He explained the rules to me, showed me the customized
Smith & Wesson K-frame revolver which won the competition, and even took me to the range to try the revolver out. I
was soon hooked and eventually spent over a thousand dollars having my own competition revolver built. After a lot of
practice, and some invaluable tips from my friend and a
local gunsmith, I won a few trophies myself.

So, there I was, trained in karate, and I could shoot the
eyes out of a gnat, if gnats have eyes, at twenty paces. I was
ready for a rematch with that guy who had beat me up four
years earlier. Fortunately, he had moved to Minnesota, and
I never saw him again.

At 6:30 Wednesday morning I was pouring my second
cup of coffee, and Sherry and Pam were making last-minute
decisions on which sweaters they would wear, when Julie
yelled for help from the front room. Sherry would have
beaten me through the door but I had her blocked off. As
we burst through into the living room, Julie ran toward us,
eyes large with fright.

"What's wrong?" Sherry and I said, simultaneously.

"There's a huge, horrible man on our front porch. I
think he's trying to get in." The door bell rang.

thinks I'm doing it on purpose."

"Girls are nice, but you must get a lot of enjoyment out of your sons. Ball games and such."

"Yes. Yes, it is fun. I don't get to see them as often as I should. Or Crystal either. My wife."

For a very brief moment, thinking of his family, this huge rock of a man seemed to visibly soften around the edges, and my imagination suddenly went into overdrive trying to find an image of a woman who would warm to him, share his bed, and bear his children. (There would come a time, lying in our own bed, when Sherry would inform me in no uncertain terms that Sweet had qualities that would capture the heart of many, many women, given the right circumstances. I took her word for it.)

"Sorry about the hour. You said early." He didn't sound sorry.

"No problem, we're early risers. You want it in detail, or the highlights?"

We spent the next twenty minutes going over everything that had happened. We were interrupted only once, when Pam came in carrying a tray with the coffee pot and two cups, closely followed by Julie carrying a second tray of assorted rolls and donuts. They both wanted to linger and listen, but Sherry anticipated that and called them back to the kitchen before I had to shoo them away.

Sweet was a good listener and took very few notes. He let me talk it all the way through to last night before he asked any questions, and he seemed to accept my version of events without reservation. I thought briefly that I would like to watch him work an interrogation. As a spectator, never the subject.

If he had any ideas of his own, he kept them to himself. Naturally that irritated the hell out of me, but there wasn't much I could do about it. It simply isn't police policy to spill their guts to civilians.

Just as we were finishing, as though they had listened from the next room, Sherry and the girls joined us. Sherry made small talk, putting Sweet at ease and leading him into a discussion of street crime, which he toned down considerably in regard for the tender ears in the room. The girls were a little distant, literally, at first, but soon they were charmed by the quiet gravel voice and moved in closer. I realized Pam, more reserved than her sister, was sitting on the floor at my feet gazing up into the Detective's square face, while Julie was perched on the arm of Sweet's chair, giggling like a . . . well, like a schoolgirl. Maybe it's his cologne.

When Sherry announced it was past time to leave for school, the girls were disappointed, but Sweet seemed almost eager as he announced he would have to move his car out of her way, and that he had to leave anyway. After a flurry of sweaters, books, handshakes, and good-byes, the house was suddenly very quiet as I poured another cup of coffee, ate a second donut, and wondered what the hell I was going to do next. I had to think about starting the Cook surveillance, but I wasn't eager to turn loose of Holloway. Not until I knew why he had been killed.

I spent the morning straightening up the office, cleaning out drawers, and organizing files. Those are all things I can do while thinking about something else. The only problem was, I didn't really have a place to start thinking.

At 10:00 A.M. I decided, since my brain didn't seem to want to work on my own problem, maybe I should put it to work on something else. I left the house and drove to Riverside Hospital. The woman at the reception desk in the main lobby directed me to the Security Office, where I found

Annabelle Hicks, Chief of Security for the hospital complex. "Good morning, Juicy Fruit," I greeted her warmly. Annabelle and I had a history.

"This ain't high school no more, C.J., and I ain't been called Juicy Fruit since I stopped car-hopping at Weber's Root Beer Stand. How the hell have you been? Sit down, sit down. Haven't seen you since reunion. Damn, that was four years ago. Don't seem possible, does it?" She was as talkative as ever, and as impressive. Annabelle had been six feet two inches tall since she was in the ninth grade. In junior high, she had been shunned as a freak by boys and girls alike. In high school, however, she had filled out, rounded out, and learned how to take advantage of her size. She had been a red-headed bombshell, six feet two inches of hot flesh. She always wore dresses to school, as tight and as short as the powers-that-be would allow. Back then her hair was always combed, her makeup was always perfect, and her favorite form of entertainment was to tease the boys into full erection, and then leave them to suffer. She was very successful at it.

I dropped into a plastic-covered chair in the corner of her small, spartan office and looked across the room at a bank of five TV monitors mounted on the wall. Each monitor gave a different black-and-white view of various security-sensitive areas around the hospital, and each monitor changed to a different camera view every fifteen seconds.

"You into voyeurism these days, Annabelle?"

"Damn right. Talk about safe sex, that's about as safe as you can get," she grinned, and suddenly I could see the same teenage redhead who had the entire male student body of Will Rogers High School tripping over their own feet for three years running. "All right, C.J., what's up? You didn't come by here to talk about old times."

"No, Annabelle, I didn't, but once in a while I think back to those days, and I still get a little tingle at the base of my spine." I rolled my eyes and heaved a nostalgic sigh. I, too, had been six feet two inches tall in high school, and during our senior year, Annabelle and I had been drawn to each other by our height as much as anything else. We had spent four wonderful months together, with our classmates cheering us on and predicting a gaggle of basketball playing offspring resulting from our union. The next two months, however, had turned into the battle of the giants, and looking back on it, I suppose we were both lucky to get away without serious injury. Annabelle had displayed a temper to match her hair color, and her passion in love was surpassed only by her passion in anger.

"We did have some times, didn't we C.J.? If you hadn't been just too damned impossible to live with, it might have developed into a long-term thing. As it turned out, you probably wouldn't have been any worse than my first husband."

"How is old Freddie these days?"

"He's dead. He's the one you met at the reunion, but he was my second husband. The first was Bubba Clay." She reminisced for a moment. "He's dead, too. I guess I've been pretty hard on husbands. How's your stamina these days, Carl?"

"Sorry, Annabelle, I don't have any at all. My wife used it all up."

She laughed, slapping the desk top. "That does surprise me, C.J. As I remember, she's just a little thing." Annabelle leaned back in her chair, put her feet up on the desk, and studied the tips of the four-hundred-dollar snakeskin cowboy boots she had started wearing to make herself even taller. She probably could have worn one of my suits without much alteration, but at the moment she was wearing a Security Officer's uniform, complete with badge and holstered 9mm automatic. She had gained weight since high school, probably topping out at over two hundred pounds, but the shoulder length hair was as red as ever, and the piercing eyes were just as green. She had gone into security work not long out of high school, starting out as a bodyguard for wealthy men who enjoyed having her around as much for her looks as for her abilities as a bodyguard. I was very much aware of her abilities, since she had joined Roger Graye's karate school during my third year there. She had advanced rapidly, due more to her persistence than to her size, but size helped, of course. It occurred to me that she would have been a great match for Detective Albert Sweet. She suddenly interrupted my daydreaming with a concise, to-the-point question.

"What the hell are you doing here, C.J.? I mean, I enjoy a visit from an old friend as much as anybody, but you haven't said a dozen words to me in as many years."

"I'm sorry, Belle, it just seems there isn't enough time anymore to do all the things we'd like to do. I'm more or less on a case. Not a big case, I'm just looking into a situation for a friend. I was hoping you could help me."

"Help you what?" She didn't sound eager.

"A young man by the name of Tal Adams was in here a few days ago having X-rays of his legs. He's a paraplegic. When he got ready to leave, they couldn't find his battery-powered wheelchair. The chair was a gift, and means a lot to him. He asked me to try to locate it for him."

"Damn. Damn it to hell! I knew this was going to happen sooner or later."

"Knew what? I'm not trying to cause trouble, or anything. I just want to help the kid get his wheelchair back."

"No, not you, Carl. At least not you specifically. I mean I knew that it would leak out eventually. See, that kid's wheelchair wasn't the first thing to come up missing. Somebody's had us running in circles around here for over two months. We've been trying to keep it quiet, but you know how it is. With this many people involved, I'm surprised it's taken this long. Up till now, all the things taken have belonged to the hospital. That wheelchair was the first item stolen from a patient."

"What else is missing?"

"What isn't, is more like it." She removed a sheet of paper from one of the in-out trays on her desk, and passed it across to me. "That's just the stuff we know about. The date in the second column is the day someone first noticed the item was missing. Only God and a really warped thief knows when they were actually taken."

I glanced at the sheet casually at first, then had to do a double-take.

1	gurney	7/4
10	sets of bed sheets	9/8
8	pillows	9/8
1	oxygen tank with mask	9/9
1	complete set of surgical instruments	10/14
8	surgical gowns, assorted sizes	10/14
3	boxes surgical masks (36)	10/14

2	stethoscopes	10/14
3	boxes cotton swabs (300)	10/15
2	clipboards	10/15
1	kidney dialysis machine	10/16
1	iron lung	10/16
6	rape test kits	10/16
5	boxes ballpoint pens	10/16
1	blood pressure monitor	10/16
15	battery-powered thermometers	10/16

At the bottom of the list someone had written in, "one battery-powered wheelchair, property of Talmidge Wayne Adams, patient." I studied the list for a few minutes, and when I looked up Annabelle asked, "Well, what do you think, Sherlock? See any pattern?"

"Obviously the guy is playing doctor somewhere, or else he's getting ready to open his own hospital. How the hell did he get all that out of here with your security system in place?"

"That, my friend, is exactly what the Board of Directors wants to know, and if I can't come up with a good answer, I may be hitting you up for a job before long."

"Are the cops working on it?"

"They say they are. It's probably not a high priority for

them. At least not yet. A few influential people in town are starting to make noise and demand action from the Chief of Police. They may even get results, in a year or two."

"You must have some idea, Annabelle. You're not new at this."

"Hell, I've got all kinds of ideas. I'm sure it's someone on the staff, someone who works here. They'd have to, to be able to get around well enough to gather up that haul, even over a two-month period. I've spent hours going over employee lists, but nothing's jumped out at me. As for how they got it out, your guess is as good as mine. That damn iron lung alone is almost ten feet long, five feet high, and weighs hundreds of pounds. It's on wheels, but you don't just push something like that out the front door without being noticed. The kidney dialysis machine isn't as big, but it's almost as heavy. The rest of the stuff could have walked out in someone's pockets, except for the pillows and the oxygen tank. But stuff is going in and out of this complex all the time, damn near twenty-four hours a day. There are towns in this state that don't use as much equipment, food, and supplies as we do. I tell you, it's got me stumped. Hell, I can't even figure out a motive. I suppose they could sell the machines, but what are they going to do with three hundred cotton swabs, and clipboards, and ballpoint pens, for God's sake?"

"Yeah. There's something else a little strange about this list. Not what's on it, but what isn't." I glanced up to see Annabelle watching me closely. "No drugs. No controlled substances, no medicines of any kind. You'd think that would be the first thing someone would steal around here."

"Give the man a cigar. You're right. Always before, when we've had problems with stealing, it's damn near always been drugs. But not this time. We've kept close track.

Nothing's missing, beyond the usual sloppy records losses. What do you make of that, Carl?"

"I don't. It doesn't make sense. Can I keep this list?" She nodded, and I folded the sheet up and slipped it into my pocket. "Well, I'm glad it's your problem and not mine."

"Come on, Carl. I thought it maybe was your problem now. You say the Adams kid is a friend of yours?"

"Yes, a good friend. But I was just going to ask around, check to see if the chair had turned up. I don't have time to start a long investigation. I've got problems of my own right now."

"Yeah, I read about you capping Jimmy. That must have been tough on you. You two were pretty close, weren't you? I never did understand that, you know? I always thought he was a little creep. Looks like I was right. Why'd he do it?"

"I don't know, Belle. That's what I'm trying to find out."

"Do me a favor, C.J., for old time's sake? You've got sources all over town. While you're out there snooping around, could you see if you can find out anything about medical supplies showing up in weird places? I wouldn't expect you to follow up on anything, just give me a call. Okay?"

"Sure, Juicy Fruit. Anything for 'old time's sake,' as you put it." After a few more nostalgic stories and a tentative handshake, I left her there in that drab little office, decorated only by closed circuit TV monitors. She was staring at them, but I had an idea whatever she was seeing happened twenty-five years and fifty pounds ago, in happier times.

Back at the house I telephoned Tal and suggested he use his magic machine to check sales of used or discount medical equipment and supplies. I've heard the modern day thief often finds a market for his goods on the Internet. I read him the list of stolen items and he said he'd get on it. He also said he might have something for me relating to my own problem a little later. Encouraged, and wanting to help Tal out in return, I called a few sources I had developed over the years and asked them to keep their eyes and ears open for any hot medical supplies on the street. I also checked with several pawn shop owners I know, and they assured me they would call if anything on the list showed up. After that, I spent some time looking out the little window of my office. It didn't help. One minute I would be thinking about medical supplies and wheelchairs, and the next minute all I could think of was Jimmy, lying at my feet.

At 2:00 P.M. Tal called with the best news I'd had in a long time. "Well, I still have a few things to check," he hedged, "but you might be able to use this. Holloway filed an earlier claim, same type of injury. This was two years ago. And he had company. It seems he was joined in the suit by a woman named Chris Yates. She was injured, supposedly, in the same accident. They each filed for damages, they each had the same lawyer and the same doctor. I find that interesting, don't you?"

"I would say so. Do you think you can find her for me?"

"I already have. Got a pencil?"

Tal proceeded to dictate his report to me over the phone, promising he would follow up with a printout as soon as he had finished his research. Then he read off an Oklahoma City address and phone number, adding, "That's an unlisted phone number. Don't tell her where you got it."

"Thanks, Tal. Send me a bill, and in thirty or sixty days

Friends and Other Perishables

send me a reminder." I could hear him laughing before he hung up.

I had to call the number five times before I reached her. After spending several minutes explaining who I was, I then had to spend even longer convincing her to see me. We agreed on 9:00 the following morning. I wished her a good day, but she didn't return the sentiment.

The next morning I left the house at 7:00 A.M. to drive to Oklahoma City, about an hour and a half away using the Turner Turnpike. Before I left, I swapped the Milt Sparks belt holster for a Jackass shoulder rig. Shoulder holsters are more comfortable for long trips sitting in a car. I would soon learn of another benefit they offer, as well.

There has always been a more-or-less friendly rivalry between Oklahoma City and Tulsa, probably because they are the two largest metropolitan areas in the state, and we are always competing for tourists and new businesses moving into the area. Maybe I have developed some sort of prejudice against our capitol city, but whether it's prejudice or just my imagination, I have a terrible time finding my way around that damn city. They use what should be a pretty simple addressing system, with some street names using the suffix designation NW, NE, SW, or SE, indicating the particular quarter of the city where that street address may be found.

But then they have Grand Boulevard, which runs in a circle completely around the downtown area. I mean, how can you find an address on a street that runs in a circle? I spend a lot of time looking at Oklahoma City maps.

As I neared the address Tal had listed for Chris Yates I noticed a bright new silver 280Z parked in the driveway. A little girl was stuffing something in the trunk. At least I thought she was a little girl until she straightened up and turned around. She looked like something you would expect to see in a porno movie about a girl's school and a lecherous professor. She had the face of a fifteen-year-old and the body of a five-hundred-dollar call girl. The cold morning air had the usual effect, as evidenced through the thin halter top she wore over faded jeans. The blue black of the top matched the shade of her hair, which was cut short, with thick bangs chopped off just above the eyes. If she'd stood still, you would have sworn she was made of porcelain.

I parked the van in front of the modest brick house and crossed the yard, trying hard not to stare. I probably did anyway, but stares were something she would have to get used to.

"Miss Yates? I'm Carl Jacobs."

"Mr. Jacobs, I know I agreed to speak with you this morning, but I'm afraid I won't have time now. Something has come up."

I swallowed hard and reminded myself I was a gentleman. "This is very important, Miss Yates. And I've driven a long way to get here, on time and alone. You made the rules and I followed them. Surely you can spare me a few minutes."

"Mr. Jacobs, two hours ago I got word that my father has had a heart attack. I have exactly forty-two minutes to reach the airport and catch my flight to Chicago. If you want to talk to me today, you can ride to the airport with me, but that's the best I can do."

"Then that's what I'll do."

She slammed the trunk shut and slid in behind the steering wheel. It was a struggle but I managed to fold myself up enough to get into the passenger seat. She wasted no time firing up the powerful little engine, slammed the manual shift into reverse, and we were six blocks away before she spoke.

"I have to stop for gas. So, what exactly do you want to know about Dennis and me?"

"I'm investigating a bodily injury claim Mr. Holloway filed a few months ago. He says he was injured in an automobile accident. He says he has trouble walking, bending, the usual things. As I told you last night, I checked records and found he was similarly injured two years ago in another automobile accident. The accident report listed you as a witness and a passenger in his vehicle. I want you to tell me about it."

She didn't answer right away. She stared straight ahead, concentrating on her driving, which was just as well since we were at least 20 mph over the posted limit.

"It sounds like you already know everything I do. What can I say about it? We had an accident and Dennis was hurt. It happens." Her voice was calm and level, but I noticed her hands tighten on the steering wheel.

"You were hurt, too. Back, wasn't it?"

"Yeah, my back. But I'm okay now."

"Who was your doctor? Carlyle, same as Holloway's?"

"Yeah, I think so."

"And the attorney, Ridgeway, represented you both in the lawsuit didn't he? How did you come to hire him?"

"That was two years ago. How should I remember?"

She braked hard and swung left across two oncoming lanes of traffic into a full-service gas station. I decided to shut up and let her simmer for a few minutes. She asked the attendant to fill it up and check the air in the front left tire, which he reluctantly agreed to do. When he was finally through and she handed him her credit card, he sighed as a subtle way of complaining about having to go all the way inside to stamp the ticket. These days full service doesn't include smiles.

"Look, Mr. Jacobs, you might as well know. I talked to Mr. Ridgeway last night after you called. He said I shouldn't talk to you at all. But since you made the trip all the way out here to see me . . . I should have called you and canceled. This morning I was worried about my father, and I forgot all about you. I don't know anything. I'm okay now, and for all I know, so is Dennis. I haven't seen him for months. When I found out he was married, I stopped seeing him. I have no intention of ever seeing him again, and I have no idea where he is, or what he's doing."

"He's not doing anything, now. He's dead. Someone put two slugs through the back of his head." So, I'm not very subtle. Sometimes it works, sometimes it doesn't. This time it didn't. Aside from a noticeable clenching of jaw muscles, she might have been trying to decide what to wear to the prom.

While I was waiting for her to say something, a gray mini-van pulled up on the far side of the gas pumps, facing the other way. The guy behind the wheel leaned out of the window and asked if we could help him find an address. Chris said she'd try, and I got the impression she was grateful for the interruption. He got out of the van carrying an unfolded map, and walked over to her door. He rested his left arm on the car top and leaned down to look through the window, then glanced over at me, startled.

"Are you bleeding, Mister?" There was real concern in his voice. The bastard.

As Chris turned to look at me, he raised his right hand and pointed the pistol. It looked like a .22 caliber automatic, with a long silencer screwed onto the end of the barrel. I managed to get my hand under my jacket, almost reaching the .45 before he fired.

Even with the silencer, in the confines of the little car the shot sounded like a loud hand-clap. The slug went through the back of my hand and into my chest. The small caliber was still enough to stun me, and push me back against the door. I couldn't move, but I could watch as he turned the pistol toward Chris, pushed the muzzle against her forehead, and pulled the trigger. Her head snapped back and he had to reach in to put a second round through her temple. He seemed pleased with the results. He was smiling as he turned back toward me and fired two more times.

I was lucky on the last two. He was trying to put them into my chest where he thought the first one had gone, but he couldn't see the .45 under my coat. The slugs smashed into the handle of the large pistol and stopped without penetrating. The impact was enough to get quite a reaction out of me, so he thought I was finished. Hell, I thought I was finished.

I saw him walk back to the mini-van, climb in, and slowly drive away. The pain in my chest and ribs was a growing fire, and I wished it would spread, because my feet and hands were cold . . . so cold.

CHAPTER EIGHT

Sometimes when you regain consciousness the mind plays games, and it takes a while to figure out where you are. This time wasn't like that. Hospitals have unique smells and sounds, so even before I opened my eyes I knew where I was. And why. I was trying to remember exactly what he looked like when the door opened and a plump little nurse walked in. A lot of nurses are overweight and smoke too much. Pressures of the job, I guess, but you'd think, of all people, they'd know better.

"Are you finally awake? Can you tell me how you feel?" Her cheerful voice didn't match my mood, but it was part of her job and I didn't hold it against her.

"I'm cold. My mouth tastes like someone else's foot. How bad is it?"

"Your doctor is down the hall. I'll let him know you're awake. There are no restrictions on your diet. Are you ready for breakfast?"

"Yes. That sounds good, thanks."

She hesitated, looked at her feet a few times, then said, "The woman you were with . . ."

"Yeah, I know. I know."

"I think your wife is in the coffee shop. I'll send for her."

"My wife is here?"

"Of course. She's been here every minute. We couldn't run her off if we tried."

"How long have I been out?"

"They brought you in yesterday morning. You've been here almost twenty-four hours. ICU sent you down to us about six hours ago." She spun on squeaky shoes and almost knocked Sherry over as they danced around each other in the doorway.

"Hi." Her voice was hoarse, and broke a little. Her hair was mussed, her eyes were swollen, and her nose was red. She was beautiful.

"Hi, yourself. You look terrible. A little rest would probably help."

"Yeah, I know. I'll get caught up on sleep after I divorce my husband."

"Not working out, is he?"

She crossed the small room slowly, her eyes damp, hands at her waist clutching a small black purse that didn't match the red sweater, or the print house dress, or the scuffed brown loafers.

"He doesn't keep his promises. He promised me he wouldn't get shot again." Pausing next to the bed she gazed lovingly into my eyes and said, "Is there any part of your body that doesn't hurt? Some part that I can kick, very hard?"

"No. Did you say kick, or kiss?"

I couldn't put my arms around her because my left was hooked up to a plastic tube and bag hanging from a stainless-steel tree next to the bed, and my right was too damn heavy to lift. But we managed. And she didn't hurt me, much.

The doctor eventually came, along with the plastic tray of plastic-flavored eggs, and while Sherry buzzed around him getting madder and madder at having her questions ignored, he poked, prodded, sniffed, and generally made a nuisance of himself. Then he gave us all the information he thought necessary.

One bullet had gotten to me, and as I had thought, it

was only a .22 caliber, but those little bastards can be nasty. This one had been a hollow-point. It had passed through the web of skin between my right thumb and forefinger, and into the left side of my chest, breaking a rib. At that point it started disintegrating, as hollow points usually do. The bulk of the slug passed from left to right across my chest just under the skin, leaving particles of lead in its path. It had stopped short of emerging on the right side, so they had to cut to remove it. They also had to make several minor incisions to remove the small fragments.

My hand hurt like hell, but he said it would heal a lot sooner than my chest because it was relatively clean. Most of the pain in my chest seemed to be from a large bruise on my left side not far from the entry wound, and about the size and shape of the handle of my automatic. I made a mental note to write the Colt company and thank them for putting together a sturdy pistol. It had stopped the two follow-up rounds from punching through to my chest. So, one large bruise, one entry wound, and several surgical cuts across my chest, as well as the entry and exit wounds on my left arm. Not pretty.

The doctor suggested I might want to consider a new line of work. Then he left with Sherry on his heels asking about my release and just exactly what-the-hell was the little red pill, and how soon should the bandages be changed, and something else I couldn't quite make out as her voice receded down the hall. Or maybe my attention lagged a little, or maybe I dozed . . .

Jimmy and I, walking home from a movie, later than we should have been because we've stayed to see the cartoon a second time. We hurry, taking a short cut through the alley behind Martha's Deli—an alley we've been through hundreds of times before. It's a back yard to us, like a park. A playground. Only this time it's dark, and there is something there besides the trash cans. Something besides the rats eating on dead cats. Something . . . no, someone! There are two of them. Dirty. Mean drunk. They're talking nasty, saying they're going to do bad things to us. Jimmy's scared. Me too. The ugly one reaches for Jimmy, and I jump in between, pushing Jimmy back. Grab the little bastard. Run Jimmy! Jimmy running, yelling. Smart-assed kid, you'll do. The fat one holds me from behind, arm across my throat. The ugly one slaps me. I can smell the whiskey on his breath as he laughs and unbuckles his belt . . .

They allowed me to transfer to a Tulsa hospital the following morning, but I slept through most of the trip in the ambulance. Sherry's father had driven her down, and she drove my van back and met us at Saint Francis. Even with Sherry's constant attention I spent another two days hospitalized, fighting a fever, a minor infection, and a head cold I never would have caught at home. It was a twilight time for me, and I don't remember all of it. One point that stands out clearly in my mind is lunch time on the second day. Sherry was seated on the edge of my bed trying to seduce me into taking one more bite of applesauce, when the door opened. My foul mood vanished when I looked up to find Pam and Julie standing in the doorway peering anxiously into the room, not really knowing what to expect. They were holding hands.

As Sherry motioned the girls closer, I noticed a very large shadow hovering behind them. Sergeant Albert Sweet, unobtrusive as ever. After getting Sherry's approval, he had picked up the girls at their grandparents' and escorted them to the hospital, then arranged for them to get into the room long enough to see for themselves that I was okay. We had a brief, warm, and teary family reunion, and the girls were reassured. Sweet insisted on waiting out in the hall. I haven't yet thought of a way to repay him, but I'm working on it.

Just as all good things must come to an end, so must all bad things. They finally let me go home. Sherry played nurse to the hilt. She fussed and scolded, doled out pills, and dutifully recorded temperatures and pulse rates just like the pros in the hospital. I did notice quite a difference, however, when it came to the alcohol rubdowns.

It was a day later before Sherry would let me out of the house, and then only as far as the back porch, where I spent almost an hour in our most comfortable lawn chair, wrapped up in my robe and a blanket. Part of the time I watched a small flock of birds fighting for position on the winter bird feeder Sherry keeps filled with sunflower seeds. For the rest of the time I was planning a murder.

Of course, I didn't call it a murder while I was planning it. I thought of it more as an execution. I would execute him for killing Dennis Holloway and Chris Yates. It wouldn't be right for me to execute him simply because he shot me once and then tried to shoot me two more times. I couldn't kill the son-of-a-bitch just because of how I had felt as I watched him point the little automatic at me and pull the trigger while I sat there like a stump, helpless, worthless. Afraid. No, of course not. That would be childish of me.

But now I had, if not a plan, at least a goal. I was going to commit an execution. All I had to do was find him.

The next morning I telephoned Sweet and told him I was up and around, in spite of Sherry's objections, and that I had news for him. He invited me to drop by the station as

Friends and Other Perishables

soon as I felt like it. I not only felt like it, I was eager to do so, since I had recognized the face behind the .22 automatic as the same face that had walked into Holloway's apartment building carrying the bug sprayer. Within the hour I planted myself in the chair next to Sweet's gray metal desk. He didn't look up.

"It was the exterminator," I said to the top of his head.

"Yeah, I know. How's the arm? And the hand? And the chest?" Sweet didn't even look up from his desk when he said it.

"We're all fine, thank you. How the hell do you know who it was, and what do you need me for?"

"You told me in the Oklahoma City hospital. It was before you were completely awake, so you don't remember. I had to fight off a very nasty nurse to question you, but you told me everything. If you hadn't, do you think I would have let you lie around the house for four days without interrogating you? Not to mention Fry, who was prepared to storm your house and mace Sherry if he had to, just so he could question you himself, until I passed the word to him. Besides, the apartment manager finally got back from a two-week Gay Pride camp out in Colorado, and she advised us that the building had been sprayed two weeks earlier, and neither she nor anyone else had ordered a second spraying. Ergo . . . it must have been the exterminator."

"Ergo . . . why do you want me down here when I could be home watching Perry Mason reruns?"

"Mug books. Several of them. I want to test your powers of observation. You've seen him in person twice, and that's not fair. I want to see him too, in the flesh, so to speak. You tell me who he is and I'll go look at him."

"Sweet, something has been bothering me. How did this bastard know about the Yates girl? I can guess, but I don't know for sure. Did he follow me to her? I know he followed us from her house to the gas station. That's the only way he could have known where we were. But what was he doing there in the first place? Was he after me, and she got in the way, or was it the other way around?"

"You first. What is your guess?"

"She told me she had spoken with the attorney, Ridgeway, after she talked to me. That's the only way anyone could have known I was going to see her."

"Yeah, that makes sense. She called him to find out what she should say to you, to keep their stories straight. Then Ridgeway phoned the hit man. Except that we can't prove any of it. We can't be sure she didn't talk to someone else, someone she didn't tell you about."

"Actually, Sweet, we can't even be sure he was after her. He may have been after me, and took her out to eliminate a witness."

"No, it's a little more complicated than that. I think it goes like this. We checked out your story about the girl's father having a heart attack. It never happened. The old boy is doing fine, or at least he was before he heard his daughter had been killed. We assume the hit man, or whoever hired him, called Yates with the story about her father so she would go to Chicago and be out of your reach. But she took too long to get packed and ready. You arrived before she left, and so the only thing they could do was to get rid of both of you. As for you, they were simply trying again to accomplish something they had botched before. I figure the girl was a sacrifice. They decided to cut their losses. Cover their tracks, so to speak. They may be running now, or they may think the milk is back in the bottle. Or that it will be when you're taken care of."

Friends and Other Perishables

"So, if I hadn't found her and decided to question her, she might still be alive."

"Maybe. But you won't get far thinking like that."

He showed me to a small partitioned-off space with a table, a couple of chairs, and a stack of mug books, or photo albums if you're a civilian. I grumbled a bit, as all civilians do when they have to look at hundreds of pictures of assorted felons, because three out of five of them all look alike. Of course, I didn't want Sweet to know exactly how eager I was to learn the identity of my assailant. I mean, if I was going to find him and kill . . . execute him, it would help if I at least knew his name.

It took an hour and twelve minutes. I spent another ten minutes to be sure, but I could have spent ten days, and I wouldn't have changed my mind. Even in the mug shot he still had that little smirk I had memorized, while he casually put two slugs into Chris Yates. I caught Sweet's eye, and he drifted over.

"This is the one. Numb 744586-2. What kind of name is that, Russian?"

He slipped the photo out of the slot and walked across the room past his desk to a computer terminal tucked away in a corner next to a push broom and a coat rack. After lowering his considerable bulk onto an endangered swivel chair, he punched a few keys, and up popped a screen full of information about our exterminator. Since I was still an invalid, Sweet read it to me.

"Loomis, Percival G., date of birth 4-18-40, male Caucasian, 5'10", 187 pounds, brown and brown."

"Percival? A hit-man named Percival? I don't believe it."

"Well, he had a few other names he used occasionally."

"I should hope so. When my wife finds out I let myself get shot by a guy named Percival . . ."

89

"Shut up. AKA Ray Loomis, AKA Louis Ray, AKA Lou Giannetti . . ."

"Yeah, that one. That's the one I'll use when I tell Sherry."

"I'm going to tell her it was a woman."

"Hell, she'd believe that. Then she'd want to know why, and if I couldn't tell her I'd be back in the hospital."

"How are Sherry and the kids?"

"To tell the truth, they're driving me nuts with all the nursing and pampering. I have to brush my teeth while they're all sleeping, or else they would insist on doing it for me." I paused, considering, and adjusted the bandage on my right hand. "Actually, it's kind of nice."

"Yeah, it is, ain't it?" Sweet smiled in a way that told me he had gone through the same thing with his family. I wondered where he had been shot.

"What's his address?"

"Percival's?"

"No. Giannetti's."

"You want to give him another chance at you? He's probably really pissed off at you for being alive."

"You think he knows? Or really cares?"

"Well, look at it. You can identify him. Your testimony will put him away for good. I'd say you are probably right at the top of his list of unfinished business."

"So. If he's such a sorehead, I probably won't have to go to his place. He'll be coming to . . . Damn!"

"Sit down, Carl. I've asked the Tulsa police to have a car out in front of your house since you woke up in the hospital. In fact, two cars. One very visible, cruising the neighborhood, and a second, almost invisible, within shouting distance of your front door. The girls are okay."

"Just the same, I think I'll treat them to a few days in the country. Maybe they can go to Sherry's folks' cabin. Pam and Julie will love that. I may have to tie Sherry up, though. Is it against the law to tie up your own wife?"

"That depends on whose idea it was, and how soon you let her loose." Suddenly the mood changed, and Sweet became very serious.

"Knock off the nonchalance crap, Jacobs. You're not fooling anyone. You want this guy all to yourself. You think you're going out on some wild animal hunt and bag your killer before he bags you. Well you can forget it. It's our job—mine—not yours. Besides, if you kill him you'll have to prove it was in self-defense, or it would then be my job to get you."

"I think you might at least give me credit for . . ."

"For what? Having enough sense to know when to lay off? For knowing when a friend is trying to save your ass from getting blown away, or maybe locked up for a few years?" He threw the pencil he was holding across the room. He continued to glare at me as he rose—and rose—then casually walked across to get his pencil back. Detective Sergeant Boswell, whom I had met a few years ago, was talking on the phone and never missed a beat as he retrieved the pencil from his half-empty coffee cup and held it out to Sweet without looking up. I got the impression it wasn't the first time Sweet had thrown something in that room.

"Okay, Sweet. You win. I won't interfere. But you can at least let me help. I'm an experienced investigator, Sweet. I won't get in the way, I promise. You're right, of course. I want this guy. I mean, I can close my eyes and I can still smell him. He wears that cheap green aftershave, you know? The memory of that smell keeps me awake at night. Mixed with the smell of gunpowder. And the smell of my own fear."

"We all know what fear smells like, Carl, and it almost always accompanies the smell of gunpowder. But it goes away. Eventually. Fear isn't a bad thing, you know. It's something that helps keep guys like you and me alive."

Well, maybe so, but I had an idea the only thing that had kept me alive so far was dumb-ass luck.

The next two weeks were tough on everybody. I drove Tal and his computers pretty hard trying to find a lead to Giannetti. I was taking it for granted he was still in the city. I was ignoring the probability that he was using still another phony name. Tal was no help, but he showed a lot of class by not telling me to go to hell.

I kept the phones tied up pestering Sweet and any other official ear that would listen to me, wanting to know what they were doing, what they were going to do, and why no one was keeping me advised. Sweet had notified the Oklahoma City authorities about the shooter's identity, and presumably they were looking for Giannetti too. They even sent a Detective up to interview me again about the incident, but I think I asked more questions than he did. I also used up a lot of favors by contacting all of my private sources to see if they could get a line on "Percy," as I affectionately called him when no one was listening. Of course they'd never heard of him. My sources were more likely to know about scams and frauds than any homicide. They ran with a better class of crook.

When I wasn't on the phone, I was pacing the floor and snapping at the girls. Sherry refused to consider my suggestion that she and the girls go out of town for a while. The ensuing argument lasted several very tense days. Looking back I would guess Sherry was about five days from either divorcing me or locking me in a closet for the duration,

Friends and Other Perishables

when one Friday night Sweet telephoned and invited me to join him on a surveillance of an apartment complex on Riverside, where Percy was believed to be currently hanging his hat. I accepted his invitation.

Eleven hours is a long time unless you're sleeping or having fun. Sweet and I hadn't been doing either for at least that long. We had been sitting in a panel truck parked a hundred yards south of the front entrance to the Braden Apartments, where one of Sweet's informants had observed a subject he believed to be one Percival Loomis, but who had rented the furnished apartment under the name Patrick Lawson. Lawson had not been in the apartment when Sweet and a few of his friends from the Tulsa Police Department came to call the previous evening. The apartment manager knew only that his new tenant, in residence for less than three months, paid cash and didn't talk much. They found nothing useful in the apartment. Sweet said it had looked like a motel room, with no personal items except for a change of underwear and a cheap blue suit in the closet. So Sweet had established around-the-clock surveillance on the building, with the permission and the assistance of local authorities, and invited me to sit in with him on the first watch. We were due to be relieved at 8:00 Saturday morning, but the relief team had been delayed, and at 9:18 A.M. we were eighteen minutes into our twelfth hour. Fortunately Sweet's surveillance van, compliments of the city of Broken Arrow, was furnished about like mine, with all the necessities.

That helped the bladder problems but did nothing for the boredom. I sank so low as to kill time by watching a tall, skinny, very un-funny mime performing for a group of parents and young children in a nearby park. I soon realized my opinion of mimes hadn't changed over the years.

"Hey, Sweet, what's the penalty for strangling a mime?"

"I don't know. Probably nothing serious."

"I wouldn't think so. Maybe a fine, you think?"

"Maybe. You might even get away with it. Maybe no one would notice. I mean, it's not like everything would suddenly go quiet."

I treated myself to a jaw-breaking yawn and a full body stretch. "If it gets any quieter around here, I'll fall asleep. You do many surveillances, Sweet?"

"Not for the last few years. I used to do a lot of them when I worked Narcotics Division, but we don't have much call for them in Homicide. When we do, I usually let the guys with the younger kidneys handle it."

"Yeah. Unfortunately I still have to pull a lot of surveillance duty. Investigating insurance fraud almost always requires some surveillance work. Maybe I'm getting too old for it myself. It's not much fun anymore."

Sweet continued to watch the entrance to the apartment building down the street as he smiled slowly, remembering. "It can be. I was working a surveillance my first month in Narcotics. We suspected a small time pimp was going into a new line of work, using his stable to market and deliver coke. Well, one night we set up surveillance on a few of his girls, and . . . well now, who do you suppose that is?"

A taxi pulled up in front of the apartment house. The passenger stepped out, paused long enough to pay the driver, then quickly mounted the steps and disappeared inside. He was wearing jeans, a black waist-length leather jacket, and a ball cap, but I still recognized him as our subject, Percival Loomis. That is, Sweet's subject. My target. A target I wanted all to myself.

"Could be," I said, doubtfully. Sweet reached for the radio to call for backup. "Wait a minute, Sweet. Don't you think we should make sure, before you get a crowd down here?"

"I'm sure. So are you. I'm disappointed in you, Jacobs. You gave me your word." He thumbed the radio mike and called in our location, requesting a squad car to assist in serving a felony homicide warrant. Then he turned to me.

"Let me have your gun."

"What?"

"You heard me, damnit, give me your gun. Now!"

I handed over the automatic, reluctantly. Sweet briefly admired the cherry-wood grips I had installed to replace the ones damaged by Percy's .22, then stuck it under his belt. Ignoring my angry glare, he leaned back, eyes focused on the distant stoop. Neither of us had anything to say until the TPD backup unit arrived, along with Detective Fry. Fry sent one of the uniformed officers to cover the rear. The other entered through the front entrance with us. At Sweet's insistence I was last in line, and well back when Fry pounded on the apartment door and announced, "Police Officers. Search warrant. Open up!"

All hell broke loose. The door splintered as Loomis fired three rounds through it; rounds from something heavier than a .22. Fortunately we were all clear, and the only damage was to Fry's suit coat, when a sharp sliver of wood punched through his sleeve.

After we had started breathing again, the uniformed officer, Neilson, delivered a powerful front kick to what was left of the door, and all four of us rushed through, guns drawn. Well, my gun wasn't drawn, but it would have been if I could've reached it.

There was no one in the small room. The window was open, and from somewhere below we heard the sound of two closely spaced shots, followed by a third. Then silence.

Fry looked through the window, then motioned us back out the door. We raced down and around to the back. Loomis was lying on the pavement beneath the fire escape ladder. A blue steel Colt revolver lay next to him. The second uniform, revolver in his hand, was standing over the body. He was young, and scared, and he had shot and killed someone for the first time in his life.

"I had to, Sir. He shot at me. He wouldn't stop. I had to."

"That's okay, Parker. You did fine. Relax," Fry said, trying to reassure the young cop.

"I'm sorry. Really. I had to."

"Sure you did. Now holster your piece. Neilson, take him back to the unit and give him a chance to catch his breath. And call this in. Tell them we need a shooting team and EMSA down here."

"Right Sergeant. Come on, partner."

While Sweet and Fry went about their business, I stood there, looking down at the man I had been planning to execute. The cold-blooded, hired killer who robbed a small boy of his father, who smiled while he killed a beautiful girl, and who had filled me with hatred and fear. He looked like I felt. Small and all used up.

CHAPTER NINE

The same question kept circling through my mind. All right, smart guy, now what are you going to do? Followed by the same answer. Damned if I know.

"What are we going to do now?"

"Huh? What did you say, Sherry?"

"I said, what are we going to do now? Giannetti's dead, Jimmy's dead, and we still don't know why either one of them wanted to kill you. I can't even think of where to start thinking. So, what do we do now?"

"Damned if I know."

Sherry was fixing Sunday breakfast for two. She was wearing the filmy blue gown I had given her for Christmas last year, and the fact that I hadn't noticed before was an indication of how distracted I really was. That was some gown.

"What are you wearing under that thing?"

"I'm wearing the same thing I wore to sleep in. Wasn't that you beside me all night?"

"Yeah. That was me."

"Then you should know what I was wearing. Or not wearing."

"Sure. Where are the girls?"

"They ate earlier, then went to Sunday school and church with Mike and Cindy next door. They'll be gone for a couple of hours." She turned to face me, one hip cocked to the side, her fingers playing with the lace at her shoulder. "Why do you ask?"

The smile on her face was all innocence. It didn't match

the negligee. As she moved slightly, the floor-length gown separated in front, displaying a lovely bare leg all the way up to about there.

"Well . . . uh . . . I just thought that maybe we . . . I mean you're so . . . Should you be frying eggs dressed like that? I mean, if you splattered grease you might stain it, right? And besides, the loose material might brush over the flames from the stove. You could catch on fire, and I would have to jump up, rip the gown right off you, and throw you to the kitchen floor, to smother the flames with my own body."

"What flames?"

"Don't you feel flames? I was sure I . . ."

"This is an electric skillet. No flames."

"Well . . . hell."

She leaned forward, cradled my face in her hands, took a deep—deep—breath, and sighed. "Sweetheart, why are you always so lecherous in the kitchen? Now answer my question, what are we going to do?"

"Well, I think for starters we should draw the curtains and lock the back door. Then we could . . ."

Sherry laughed as she shoved me away from her and turned back to the eggs. "I'm talking about the case, Carl. Leave me alone or you'll end up with this breakfast in your lap."

"Oh, yeah, the case. Well, I still have a surveillance to work for Underhill. A guy named Cook. I guess I'll start that tomorrow." My heart wasn't in it.

"Well, that's stupid. I never thought you were a stupid man, Carl, but you sure act stupid sometimes." She dropped the plate of bacon and eggs on the table in front of me to emphasize her point, and some of the bacon slid off the plate onto the table.

"Sweetheart, stop trying to spare my feelings. If you have any thoughts you would like to share, feel free to speak right up." I retrieved the bacon and Sherry wiped the table vigorously with a paper towel, breathing heavily as much from frustration as exertion.

"My thoughts are that there is someone, or maybe several someones, out there who want you dead, and you've already been shot twice, and there are now three dead people . . . no, four, five dead people—we've got bodies scattered all over the damn city—and you're planning to go off to work tomorrow as if you hadn't a care. Now, am I wrong, or is that stupid?"

She was right, of course, but I didn't know what the hell to do. I couldn't just sit in my little office and wait for Sweet to call and tell me when everything was wrapped up and I would be safe on the streets. I couldn't go storming off into the night, armed to the teeth, to bring the bastard to justice, because the bastard was already dead. At least the only bastard we had identified. Sure it was stupid to try to lead a normal life under those circumstances, but if I was smart I would have known what to do next. A few times in the past, when I had been stumped on a case I had asked Sherry for advice, something she was always ready to offer. So I asked her politely, "Okay, smart guy, what do you think I should do next?"

And of course she replied just as politely, "Damned if I know. You're the detective, go out and detect something. Find a clue, or a footprint, or ask one of your goddamned snitches if they . . ." She remembered Jimmy, and the tears started. She quickly turned away and busied herself at the sink.

I pushed the plate of cold eggs away and rose, walking over to stand behind her at the sink, my arms around her, my face buried in her hair. It seems we spend a lot of time like that, especially in the kitchen.

"Sweetheart, I'm going to be super-careful, I promise. I'm not going to let anyone do anything to me, or to my family. I'm through being the victim."

She turned in my arms to face me. "Please do be careful, Carl. The girls and I need you very much. That's one thing we all have in common. We all three desperately need you."

That's one thing we all have in common. I repeated it to myself, then did some hard thinking. Jimmy Jay, Philip Foster, Dennis Holloway, Chris Yates, Percy, and me. What did all of us have in common, besides being dead or being targeted for death, like me? Well, we were all associated in some way with insurance, or insurance companies. But hell, everyone has something to do with insurance, in one way or another. That was a pretty broad category. I mean, we all probably ate mashed potatoes, too, but I doubted that was relevant.

Foster and I were investigators, Jimmy had filed a false claim, and it was a pretty good bet Holloway and Chris Yates did also. Linking fraud investigation and phony claims together certainly didn't stretch the imagination. But I still needed to narrow it down a little. Maybe a lot.

Jimmy killed Foster, and tried to kill me. I killed . . . Percy killed Holloway and Yates, and tried to kill me. Jimmy and Percy, working together? Not likely. Percy was a pro, Jimmy was a . . . what? Victim? Errand boy? Hired hand.

Jimmy and Percy working for the same person? More likely. Probably. Holloway and Yates working together in the fraud? Certainly. What about the doctor and the attorney they used in their civil action? Who were they again? Carlyle, and the attorney was, uh, Ridgeway. One of them, or maybe both of them, could be the brains behind an insurance fraud scheme. Phony claims, supported by phony medical reports, filed by an unscrupulous attorney, with a share of the proceeds going to everyone. Whoa!

How much would a "share" be? I mean, looking at the dollar amount of the claims, when you split that three, four, five ways, and pay hospital and medical bills, you don't get much. Probably not enough to justify multiple killings. The biggest share would have to go the "accident victim" to make it worth their while, lying around the house for weeks, missing work, acting crippled whenever anyone was looking, never going out of the house without a cane, or crutches, or braces, or a wheelchair. So, that wouldn't leave much for the masterminds. A few bucks here and there, unless . . . Unless they pulled the same stunt over and over. A few bucks here and there and here again, and over yonder . . . it would all add up eventually. I suddenly remembered a statistic I had read some time back which stated that insurance fraud was a five-billion-dollar-a-year industry.

I needed some more information, and I knew where to get it: my pal, Tal, who, by the way, answers the phone in a rather abrupt manner. "What?"

"Tal, this is Carl. You got a minute?"

"Sure, but let me put you on hold for a minute. I'm on the other line to Italy."

While I was waiting, I wondered if computers in Italy could speak English.

"I'm back, Carl. What can I do for you?"

"Grab a sharp pencil and take down these names. James Walter Jay, Philip Foster, Dennis Holloway, Chris Yates, Carlyle and Ridgeway, the doctor and attorney you had in your report on the Yates/Holloway civil suit, Percival G. Loomis, AKA Ray Loomis, AKA Louis Ray, AKA Lou

Giannetti. You've already given me some information on a few of those. I need more. What I want you to do is a complete check of civil and criminal records on all those names, throughout Oklahoma and surrounding states, for the previous five or ten years, whatever is available. I need to know what all those people have in common, who knew each other, stuff like that. You might focus on insurance claims, civil suits, that sort of thing. You got all that?"

"I record all calls. I've got you on tape."

"Yeah? Is that legal?"

"Sure. I think. I suppose you want all this stuff tomorrow?"

"I need it now. If I needed it tomorrow, I would have called you tomorrow."

"Well, I can give you as much as I have now, and the rest as it comes in."

"Okay, great. Go ahead." He hung up on me.

We spent the afternoon as a family, getting caught up on chores around the house. The girls raked the yard, Sherry washed windows and did laundry, and I painted the spare room. After we all got cleaned up, we went out for hamburgers and a movie. We usually rent a video or two on weekends, but sometimes it's more fun to go out to a movie theatre together. Besides, the popcorn is better.

Monday was a miserable day. After Sherry and the girls left, I spent two hours sitting in the little office, re-hashing everything that had happened—much as I had the day before, with the same results.

At 9:30 A.M. I left the house and drove to Owasso, just fifteen minutes north of Tulsa, to begin my preliminary investigation and surveillance of Nelson Cook, the guy who slipped on a grape in his local grocery and had collected, to date, over thirty-five thousand dollars in medical bills and liability insurance benefits, and whose attorney had recently announced they were seeking additional compensation for "mental stress" resulting from his injuries.

The address I had for Cook turned out to be an eight-unit two-story apartment building. I interviewed a few neighbors, using what we investigators call an "indirect approach." That means we look them in the eye and lie about who we are and what we are doing. I eventually determined Cook lived in unit "D" on the second floor and drove a black 1980 Ford two-door sedan which he parked on the street. There wasn't any black Ford parked nearby, so I went up and knocked on the door of unit "D" to see if anyone was home. There was no answer. I went back to my surveillance van and set up about a block away, from where I could watch the front entrance. While I was loading a new tape into my video camera, I had a horrible feeling of deja-vu, and I envisioned Mr. Cook lying on his living room floor in front of the TV with two .22 slugs in his head.

I lasted three hours in the van before the vision of a murdered Nelson Cook became so strong I had to find out for certain that he was still alive. I started to call the information operator to get a number for the apartment building and try to speak to the manager, but I discovered I had left my cell phone at home on the charger. I returned to the apartment building and knocked on doors until I found the building manager. I fed him a line about how I had been trying to get in touch with Cook for several days, and I was afraid there might be something wrong, because, "with his bad heart and all . . . ."

"Forget that crap, mister. I know you been all over the building asking about Cook. I don't care about that, and I don't care why you're looking for him. His problems are his. I got plenty of my own. Besides, he hasn't been here for two or three weeks. I been in his apartment. You know, checking on things. All his clothes are gone, not that he ever had much anyway. I think he pulled out, left for good."

"Any idea where he might have gone?"

"Nope. I think he has family in Tennessee, or Kentucky somewhere, but that's a guess. I'm not worried about it, his rent is paid up through the end of the month."

I handed him one of my business cards, the one that indicated I worked for a collection agency. "Would you call me if he comes back?"

"Oh, sure. You bet."

When pigs fly.

Of course I couldn't take the super's word for it. I called Tal from a pay phone, added Cook's name to the list I had given him the day before, and suggested he try the Department of Motor Vehicles first, since we knew Cook had a car. Then I wasted an hour trying to learn something from neighborhood merchants who might have had Cook as a customer. The local dry cleaner admitted knowing him, and even went so far as to check the shelves and racks of laundry waiting to be picked up, but there was nothing there for Cook. I canvassed the rest of the nearby merchants. I found very few people who would even talk to me and no one who admitted knowing Cook.

After that I went home and sulked.

Tuesday morning Tal called in his preliminary report. It was even more than I had hoped for. The attorney, Harlan Q. Ridgeway, and the good Doctor Stanley Carlyle had been "working together" for quite a while, and their track record was impressive. Tal produced a list of more than eighty-five civil suits Ridgeway had filed on behalf of suffering clients seeking damages ranging from twenty-five thousand dollars to over five hundred thousand dollars, and totaling approximately thirteen point five million. In every case, Doctor Carlyle had testified or had submitted medical records which supported the allegations of severe pain, disability, and mental anguish. What was even more interesting was the fact that there were numerous other suits filed by Ridgeway which named a second medical doctor and at least two chiropractors, while Carlyle's name showed up in suits initiated by three other attorneys. All of this activity had taken place within the previous five years.

"Tal, what sort of injuries are we talking about?"

"Well, mostly back injuries. A few head, neck, and shoulder, several hip problems, and strangely enough over two dozen emotional stress and psychological disorders resulting from minor injuries. They throw in a few phobias, and even a couple of sexual dysfunctions, with the spouses seeking compensation as well. It's quite an assortment. These guys are really creative."

"Yeah. Sounds like they have it down pat."

"The files indicate they supposedly ran every sort of test imaginable. They did a lot of psychological stuff, and in almost every case they performed something called a 'CAT scan' or MRI."

"Yeah, that figures. Actually, those are two different things. A CAT scan is done with computers and X-rays. They use it to look at cross-sections of the body, checking your organs and things for injuries or tumors, like that. The MRI, or Magnetic Resonance Imaging, uses a magnetic field and radio waves to do about the same thing, I guess. It used to be Nuclear Magnetic Resonance, but the word "nuclear" scared everybody off. It's supposed to be safer than an X-ray. For both of them they lay you down on a table, then push you into a big tube. I don't know how they work, but they must be doing something right."

"Well, however they work, they're expensive, and these guys order a lot of them. They must be making a fortune, Carl."

"That's not the half of it. You might consider the fact that the number of civil suits filed usually represent only about a third of the case load for an injury lawyer. Many cases are settled before they reach the court house."

"You mean . . . that's going to be about . . . one hundred seventy-five cases for over forty million. Wow!"

"Wow, indeed. Even if Ridgeway and Carlyle get to keep only half, that's ten million apiece, or a cool two million bucks a year. Thanks, Tal. You've been a big help. Send me a bill." I nestled the phone back on its cradle while Tal was in mid-sentence. These new figures suggested that the prize in this game was, after all, big enough to tempt some people to multiple murders.

I banged my shin on the desk, startled by the telephone ringing while my hand was still on the receiver. "What?"

"Excuse me, but you didn't let me finish."

"Sorry, Tal. Finish what?"

"My report. There is something else you might find interesting."

"Like what? What could be better than what you've already given me?"

"They own it."

"What?"

"They own it. The CAT scan place."

"What? Who does?"

"Ridgeway and Carlyle. They own Shannon Research Center, the clinic that performs all the CAT scans and MRIs they order. At an average of about fifteen hundred dollars for each exam."

Friends and Other Perishables

"The lawyer and the chiropractor? They own the clinic?"

"Right. At least they own part of it. Along with three medical doctors, four other chiropractors, and two other attorneys. That accounts for about half-ownership. The rest is owned by something called MedCon, a business or a corporation, I don't know. I'm still trying to pin it down."

"So, a guy gets hurt, his chiropractor treats him, recommends a high-dollar test, sends him to his own clinic, then recommends a good high-dollar attorney, who recommends filing a civil suit, and probably a few more tests just to be sure."

"That about covers it, Carl. I guess all they need now is their own judge."

"I don't know, kid. The way they've been doing things lately, they may soon feel the need to invest in a high-dollar funeral parlor. Thanks, Tal. I'll be in touch."

I spent the afternoon on the phone with some of my contacts, doctors and lawyers I had occasion to meet over the years. I was digging for information about Carlyle and Ridgeway. I might as well have been asking about the dark side of the moon. No one wanted to gossip about one of their own, though a few of the doctors had less than flattering things to say about the attorney, Ridgeway, and at least two attorneys were willing to bad-mouth Carlyle, the chiropractor. But it was all personal opinions, rather than facts I could use.

I couldn't come up with one shred of evidence that could point conclusively to Carlyle and Ridgeway, even though I knew, without a doubt, that they were connected either directly or indirectly to at least five deaths and three attempted murders, all three of which were directed at me. I suddenly remembered what Sherry had said just before she left for work.

"Carl, if you get a chance, would you prepare the shrimp I picked up at the market yesterday? We should have it for dinner tonight. It was fresh when I got it, but I don't think we should let it set any longer. Shrimp is just too perishable."

Perishable, I thought. Aren't we all.

When Sherry and the girls arrived home that evening, they had a surprise for me.

"It's a puppy. Isn't he cute?" That was Julie's idea of a hard sell.

Pam was more practical. "I'll take care of him, Daddy. I promise. Can we keep him?"

I looked at Sherry, accusingly, and she set me straight right away. "Don't look at me, mister. It wasn't my idea. Grandpa gave it to them."

I looked at the little stranger with a closed mind and a hard heart, but before the right words could be formed, the girls had started to romp—yes, little girls do romp—around the front room, with the delighted young dog the center of attention, and loving it. I say young dog, because I didn't want to think of it as a puppy. Puppies are lovable, cuddly little creatures that people just can't resist, and I definitely wanted to resist this one. I suppose he was cute, in a way. He looked to be part basset, with his short legs and long floppy ears. His coloring was a patchwork of brown and black, on a dirty white. He had white rings around both eyes. Eyes that seemed to be constantly sneaking a peek at me. Every time I would look at him, he would be looking at me, almost sideways, out of the corner of his eyes. His eyes were sad and thoughtful, and if I had to guess, I would say that he was thinking to himself, "You look like a man who would cook and eat dogs. I'm not going to take my eyes off you for a second." Yes, this was a dog I definitely wanted to resist. But fate was against me. Everyone seemed to forget that they had asked for permission, which I had not yet given. Sherry led the three youngsters into the kitchen, where she proceeded to feed the youngest and make him welcome. I took some pleasure in the knowledge that our dinner would include shrimp and salad, neither of which are enjoyed by dogs. By golly, at least the mutt wouldn't be begging for scraps or enjoying leftovers from dinner. Of course, that was before I found out, a short time later, that this particular dog would eat anything he could chew up and swallow—including my black leather house shoes, for which I had paid thirty-five dollars. At least the dog didn't cost anything, thanks to my father-in-law. Bless him.

That evening, after dinner, we all settled in the living room, I with the paper, Sherry with a pair of scissors and page after page of discount food coupons which she cut out and sorted, the two girls with the television, and the dog with a section of the paper I hadn't yet finished. Occasionally I would glance up and look across the room to where Jackson was lying near the fireplace, spitting out shreds of newspaper, watching me all the time. Sly dog.

The next morning had already been planned out for me weeks earlier. I was subpoenaed to appear in Worker's Compensation Court to testify and present videotape evidence I had obtained during a surveillance from almost a year before. I had been retained to conduct surveillance of an auto mechanic who was supposedly injured on the job and swore that as a result, he couldn't walk, drive a vehicle, return to his old job, or satisfy his wife in bed. My client wanted video of the claimant performing one or more of those activities. I never got video of him with his wife, but I did have about thirty minutes of him bowling in a

Wednesday night industrial league tournament.

Before I left the house, I reviewed the report and the videotape to be sure I would recognize the claimant in court. It's embarrassing when your attorney asks you to point out the person you investigated for two weeks, and you can't pick him out of a crowd.

I loaded my gear into the van, including the tape, a combination television and videotape player, and wheeled cart to carry everything, then double checked to make sure I had the TV remote control and an extension cord. I arrived in front of the Court Building by 8:00 A.M., early enough to be sure to find a parking space in the small lot. I backed into one near the double doors and began unloading my equipment. I didn't hear them behind me until the big one spoke.

"Say, guy, could you spare a buck or two so we could get some breakfast?"

I turned around, startled, to find myself confronted by two men, mid to late twenties, both with the look of street people about them. Tulsa has its share of homeless, and sometimes one or more of them will get a little aggressive with their panhandling, but for the most part, they're just trying to get by. These two appeared to be a different matter all together. The one closest to me was perhaps a full two inches taller than me, and he didn't appear to have missed too many meals. His shoulder-length hair was tangled, as was his beard. There were still leaves and grass in his hair from sleeping on the ground the night before. The other was shorter, dark, and nervous. He kept looking around, right, left, behind, all the time licking his lips. He kept both hands in the pockets of his grease-stained fatigue jacket.

I don't normally give money to people who beg for it on

Friends and Other Perishables

the street—not because I begrudge them a few dollars, but because I've always thought, if they can get it just by asking for it, what incentive is there for them to go to work somewhere? Not a popular philosophy, I know, but it works for me. This time, for some reason, I pulled out a couple of singles and held them out, saying, "Sure. It's a cold morning, I imagine you could use a cup of coffee."

The big guy wasn't satisfied. He had been checking me out, and looking over the van and the television, and apparently decided he wanted everything.

"I think you could do better than that, Pop. We'll take it all. And the keys to the van, too." He reached into his pocket and pulled out a .25 caliber automatic pistol, so small it was almost lost in his big hand. He flashed the little pistol at me and grinned, showing large gaps between his stained teeth. "Do like I say, and you won't get hurt. Hand over the keys, and climb back into the van."

A vision of my own automatic flashed through my head. It was locked in the glove box of the van. Not exactly convenient, but they don't allow firearms in Worker's Compensation Court, and I hadn't expected to be assaulted at 8:00 A.M. in the middle of downtown. My first response was anger. I was getting damn tired of being pushed around, beat up, and victimized. Besides, the son-of-a-bitch had called me "Pop."

"Come on, let's have the keys," the big guy growled. "I ain't gonna fuck around with you. You don't look near as tough as they say. And I'm sure you don't want to get your pretty suit all messy."

His partner, standing a little to one side, laughed at that, and the big guy just had to look over and smirk at his own cleverness. When he did, my temper took over. I reached out with my left hand, grabbing his right wrist to push the little pistol off-line, just in case he got off a shot. He didn't. I stepped forward on my right foot, twisted to my left, extended my right arm fully, then drove my right elbow into his ribs, just under his armpit. As the air rushed out of his lungs, I drove my shoulder under his stiffened arm, at the same time pulling down sharply on his wrist. I heard the elbow snap, and the pistol slipped out of his fingers and clattered to the sidewalk. He started screaming, and didn't stop until I swept his feet out from under him, let him fall, then banged his head against the pavement.

His partner froze, eyes wide, spittle running down his chin. I took a step toward him, and he pulled a butterfly knife from his pocket. He started through the fancy snapping and flipping maneuvers necessary to get his weapon into operation, and probably meant to intimidate anyone who was stupid enough to stand there and wait for him to finish. Instead, I drove the toe of my right shoe into his kneecap, and watched his face turn blue as he sank to the concrete surface of the sidewalk, the fancy knife still clutched, half open, in his fingers.

I had gathered up the .25 caliber automatic, a Raven, and the butterfly knife and had determined that I couldn't call the cops on my cell phone because I had left the damn thing at home again, when one of the security guards came out to see what all the ruckus was about.

"You okay, Mr. Jacobs?"

"I'm fine, George. But we'll need an ambulance for these two. Can you take care of that for me?"

"Sure thing. I'll call the cops, too."

He did so, and in a few minutes two patrol cars and an ambulance were on scene. The ambulance attendants had the two stickup men strapped down and loaded into the ambulance in short order. One of the TPD officers asked if

I wanted to press charges, and I told him I would if they didn't have anything else to hold them on.

"Are you kidding?" he asked. "They were both carrying crack and marijuana, not to mention the weapons. Besides, they're both wanted on fugitive warrants out of Oklahoma City, for armed robbery and assault. We've got plenty to hold them on."

"Then just forget about this," I said. "I'm okay, and I have to be in Court . . . Damn. Wait a minute."

I went over to the ambulance and climbed into the back. There was barely enough room to kneel down next to the little guy's cot. He was conscious, but still a little blue. I made sure the attendant and the cop were looking somewhere else when I reached out and put my fingers around the guy's throat. His eyes opened wide and he tried to say something but I squeezed a little and held my finger up to my lips. He got the idea.

"I only want to hear one thing from you, my friend. Why me? Why did you and your buddy decide to mug me, here, in broad daylight?" He just shook his head, and blinked his eyes a little faster. "I'm a little slow, but it finally sank in. Your friend made a crack about me not being as tough as he had heard. Heard from where? Who sicced you onto me?" He tried to shrug his shoulders, which loses something when you're lying flat on your back. I just squeezed a little harder, and when he couldn't get his breath, he nodded sharply, and I took my hand away.

"It was just a guy. I don't know who he was, I never seen him before. He gave us a hundred bucks. He said to mess you up a little, then haul you out into the country somewhere and . . . do you. He said we could have the van too, and anything in it. I didn't want to, but Haystack . . . that's

Haystack there. You really hurt him bad. He said we would."

"So, where did you meet this guy with the hundred bucks? And when?"

"Just this morning. We were just sitting there in the sun, trying to get warm, when he drove up and called us over."

"Sitting where, dumb ass?"

"Right over there. Across the street. That's our bridge there. Me and Haystack live there." He nodded his head toward an empty lot next to an overpass. Home sweet home.

I questioned the little guy some more, but he couldn't help me any. He couldn't even describe the man, or the car he drove, except that it was "sorta black." The cop asked again if I wanted to press charges.

"I guess not. No harm done to me, and I have to get upstairs to testify in court this morning. Let it ride. You've got enough to put them away without me."

"Fine by me. Less paperwork. You have a good day."

Well, maybe, but it wasn't starting out very well.

Some things occurring in my profession are exciting—like assault with a dangerous weapon—and many more are dull and boring, but perhaps the most boring of all is sitting in the crowded waiting room at Worker's Comp Court, 440 South Houston. Second floor, if it matters. I have often sat there, guarding a cart loaded with video equipment, waiting six or seven hours for my client, or my client's attorney, to call me into a courtroom to show the video to a judge, opposing council, and the claimant, only to be told at the last minute that the case had been settled and my presence was no longer required. Of course I get paid by the hour for sitting there all day, but I'm not sure it's worth it.

After I've read the morning paper, reviewed the case,

Haystack there. You really hurt him bad. He said we would."

"So, where did you meet this guy with the hundred bucks? And when?"

"Just this morning. We were just sitting there in the sun, trying to get warm, when he drove up and called us over."

"Sitting where, dumb ass?"

"Right over there. Across the street. That's our bridge there. Me and Haystack live there." He nodded his head toward an empty lot next to an overpass. Home sweet home.

I questioned the little guy some more, but he couldn't help me any. He couldn't even describe the man, or the car he drove, except that it was "sorta black." The cop asked again if I wanted to press charges.

"I guess not. No harm done to me, and I have to get upstairs to testify in court this morning. Let it ride. You've got enough to put them away without me."

"Fine by me. Less paperwork. You have a good day."

Well, maybe, but it wasn't starting out very well.

Some things occurring in my profession are exciting—like assault with a dangerous weapon—and many more are dull and boring, but perhaps the most boring of all is sitting in the crowded waiting room at Worker's Comp Court, 440 South Houston. Second floor, if it matters. I have often sat there, guarding a cart loaded with video equipment, waiting six or seven hours for my client, or my client's attorney, to call me into a courtroom to show the video to a judge, opposing council, and the claimant, only to be told at the last minute that the case had been settled and my presence was no longer required. Of course I get paid by the hour for sitting there all day, but I'm not sure it's worth it.

After I've read the morning paper, reviewed the case,

Friends and Other Perishables

I wanted to press charges, and I told him I would if they didn't have anything else to hold them on.

"Are you kidding?" he asked. "They were both carrying crack and marijuana, not to mention the weapons. Besides, they're both wanted on fugitive warrants out of Oklahoma City, for armed robbery and assault. We've got plenty to hold them on."

"Then just forget about this," I said. "I'm okay, and I have to be in Court . . . Damn. Wait a minute."

I went over to the ambulance and climbed into the back. There was barely enough room to kneel down next to the little guy's cot. He was conscious, but still a little blue. I made sure the attendant and the cop were looking somewhere else when I reached out and put my fingers around the guy's throat. His eyes opened wide and he tried to say something but I squeezed a little and held my finger up to my lips. He got the idea.

"I only want to hear one thing from you, my friend. Why me? Why did you and your buddy decide to mug me, here, in broad daylight?" He just shook his head, and blinked his eyes a little faster. "I'm a little slow, but it finally sank in. Your friend made a crack about me not being as tough as he had heard. Heard from where? Who sicced you onto me?" He tried to shrug his shoulders, which loses something when you're lying flat on your back. I just squeezed a little harder, and when he couldn't get his breath, he nodded sharply, and I took my hand away.

"It was just a guy. I don't know who he was, I never seen him before. He gave us a hundred bucks. He said to mess you up a little, then haul you out into the country somewhere and . . . do you. He said we could have the van too, and anything in it. I didn't want to, but Haystack . . . that's and thought through my testimony, the only thing left to do is sit and watch the people around me. Boring and depressing. So many people on crutches, canes, walkers, or wheelchairs. Others wearing neck braces or back braces or knee braces, or all three. Being the skeptic I am, I sometimes try to pick out the ones I think will leave the courtroom and head for the nearest golf course, fishing hole, or bar. On this occasion, however, I wasn't paying any attention to the crowd, and I didn't spend much time with the newspaper. I sat in a far corner, out of the traffic path, and spent my time thinking.

I thought about Jimmy Jay and Chris Yates. I thought about Percy and the young cop who had to shoot him before I could. I thought a lot about Sherry in that blue negligee. I thought about Pam and Julie, and how they would get along if something happened to their father. But most of all I thought about Doctor Carlyle and Harlan Q. Ridgeway, Attorney, and tried to figure out how in the hell I was going to nail their asses to the barn door.

At about 11:45, the attorney who was paying my hourly wage while I was doing all this thinking came by and told me I could leave, that the claimant had agreed to a settlement, and I was no longer needed. I'm sure he wasn't trying to hurt my feelings when he said it, so I didn't take offense. Besides, I would have forgiven him anyway after his parting remark, because he told me what I had to do next.

"You look like hell, Jacobs. You should see a doctor."

And that's exactly what I decided to do.

CHAPTER TEN

As soon as I got the video equipment loaded into my van I used a pay phone to call Dr. Carlyle's office. The appointment desk nurse at first insisted that there were no afternoon openings available, but with quite a bit of exaggeration about my non-existent back injury, and the comment that I was well covered with insurance, she finally agreed to slip me in between a dislocated knee and a slipped disc.

"Be here at precisely 4:15 P.M., Mr. Jacobs, and I think the Doctor can see you."

"Thank you, I appreciate that. I am in considerable pain. I'll be there."

Yeah that's right. I gave her my real name. I wasn't going to, but I remembered I would have to show her my insurance card, and of course it has my name on it. So, maybe I'm not as smart as I like to think I am.

Carlyle's office was located near 51st and Memorial Drive, in east Tulsa. At 4:10 I dragged my pain-ridden body into the large and beautifully furnished waiting room. After checking in at the front desk I had to fill out a two-page form, telling them who I was, where I hurt, and most importantly, how I was going to pay for the treatment. While I was laboriously printing all of the requested information in those impossibly small boxes, I glanced around to see who else was in pain. There was the wrenched knee sitting across the room. He was an obvious jock, wearing a sleeveless sweatshirt and denim cutoffs in spite of the thirty-degree temperatures and high winds outside. He held the

Friends and Other Perishables

two wooden crutches awkwardly, and when a horse-faced two-hundred-thirty-pound nurse came to the door and called for "Mr. Jensen," he seemed to be in real pain as he hobbled across the room and followed her down a long hallway leading to one of several treatment rooms. That left just me. Seemed like the doctor was having a slow day after all.

After completing the forms and handing them back to the receptionist, I settled down with a magazine. Before I had finished reading the article about "what women really want," I was summoned to follow a lively-looking little brunette down the same path. It was a pleasure to follow this particular nurse, since she provided an excellent view from immediately behind, if you'll pardon the expression.

She led me to a treatment room, all my own, at the far end of the hall. The first thing I noticed after we entered the small room was that she smelled good, too, and the front view was just as good as the rear, if you'll pardon the expression. All of twenty-two years old, she had a smile that was more than just a smile, and her voice was more than just a voice.

"Please remove your coat, shirt, and tie, Mr. Jacobs. You can slip this on if you like." She handed me one of those tie-on paper gowns. "I hope this fits. You're a big one. You work out too, don't you? I can always tell."

"Well, when I can. The way my back feels I probably won't be doing much of anything for a while." I emitted appropriate grunts as I removed my coat. She took it from me and hung it on a nearby hook.

"I'm sure the doctor will have you back in the saddle in no time." She smiled that smile again, and damned if I didn't feel myself start to blush.

She just stood there, smiling, with her arms crossed over

her chest, if you'll pardon . . . never mind. I removed my tie and fumbled with my shirt buttons, finally glancing at her, and then at the door. She laughed softly, actually winked, then left the room, closing the door behind her. I didn't much care if she watched me take off my shirt, but I didn't want her to see the knife hanging from a string around my neck. I had left my automatic and holster in the van, but had forgotten about the knife. As soon as the door closed, I yanked the switchblade down sharply, breaking the string, then slipped it into an inside coat pocket. I disposed of the string in a nearby wastebasket.

It was probably ten minutes later when Dr. Carlyle stepped into the small room, and I got my first look at him. I knew from Tal's report that Carlyle was forty-nine years old, had brown hair and brown eyes, weighed one hundred ninety-five pounds, and stood an even six feet tall. The report hadn't said anything about him being ugly, but he was. I don't say that in a mean way, but ugly is ugly, and this guy was . . . well, ugly. The brown hair mentioned in the report was limited to a narrow band, starting above one ear and running around the back of the skull to the other ear. The brown eyes were too far apart and bulged out below shaggy eyebrows. The nose tilted up too far, providing a repulsive view of his nostrils, to where the balance of the brown hair had migrated. He had a pronounced overbite, and his voice was about two octaves too high.

"Mr. Jacobs, is it? I'm Doctor Carlyle."

"How do you do?"

"Very well, thank you. What seems to be the problem, Mr. Jacobs?"

"Well, I bent over to pick up my newspaper this morning, and I guess I must have pulled something. I've been in pain all day, but it just seems to be getting worse."

Friends and Other Perishables

"Where, exactly, do you feel the pain?"

"In my lower back, below the belt line, mostly on the right side." I grimaced appropriately as I slowly reached behind my back and pointed to a likely spot.

"Stand up and turn around." I hadn't bothered to put on the paper gown, and his hands felt smooth and strong as he pressed hard on either side of my spine. "Does this hurt? No? How about this?"

That hurt like hell, and I told him so.

"Well, Mr. Jacobs, I think we need to get some X-rays first, then we'll have a better idea of what exactly is wrong. Just wait here for a moment and the nurse will come to get you."

He left as suddenly as he had come. I sat back down on the treatment table, which, as always, was just a little too high for my feet to reach the floor. I used to think doctors did that just to make me feel a little . . . little, while I waited for them to come back, but I suppose the real reason was so they wouldn't have to bend over so far when they finally went to work on me. I was wondering why the good Dr. Carlyle hadn't even mentioned the bandages on my arm and chest when the door opened. This time it wasn't the doctor who came back. It was the cute little nurse.

"If you will come with me, Mr. Jacobs, we'll take some X-rays and find out what you're made of." She was still smiling. Or maybe leering would better describe it.

"Should I take my clothes, Miss . . . ?"

"It's Mrs., but you can call me Joy. And you won't need your clothes for a while." Yes, definitely a leer.

We went through the procedure, just as though I was really hurting. I was hoping everyone would think I had some sort of injury that doesn't show up on X-rays. "Soft tissue" is the term. Afterwards she led me to still another room, somewhere in the back. It was a small room, dimly lit and unfurnished, except for five unusual looking beds along one wall.

"This is a roller bed, Mr. Jacobs," Joy explained, after leading me to the one in the corner. "It is motorized, and there are several rollers under the cover which massage your back and loosen you up. The doctor wants you to get the full treatment while he studies your X-rays. Please lie down with the pillow under the back of your neck. Hands at your sides, and don't cross your ankles like that. That's better. Comfy?"

"Yes, thank you, but the leather is a little cold."

"It will warm up in a minute. Trust me." Needless to say, I didn't, really.

"I'll set it on a slow roll, full length," she added. "And I think we can set the timer for fifteen minutes. We should have that much time."

After turning a few knobs and flipping switches on the side of the contraption, she pushed one last button, and suddenly there were wheels, or a series of rollers, the full width of the bed, rolling just under the surface. They started at my ankles and traveled all the way up to my neck. The motion was similar to floating on a body of water with waves washing under me. But these waves were hard, and each one generated a similar wave motion passing along my prone body. As she stood next to the bed, watching and smiling, it occurred to me that the motion was, to say the least, suggestive. Apparently the thought occurred to her, as well. And probably not for the first time.

"Fifteen minutes should be just about right." She turned her back to me, modestly, reached under her starched white uniform, and removed something sheer and silky. Then she turned around and, with what I recognized as a practiced motion, she threw one leg over the bed, and me, as though she was mounting a horse. I was startled and embarrassed, and I realized almost immediately, if I didn't get her off of me pretty soon I might start to like it.

"Miss . . . uh . . . Joy, I don't think . . ."

"You don't have to, sweet thing. Just relax and enjoy it." Her legs gripped the side of the bed as she leaned her upper body forward, pressing me down. She gently kissed the bandage on my chest, murmured "Poor baby," then continued by kissing my bare chest and on up to my neck. She ran her hands along my arms until she gripped my wrists, pushing them above my head. The damn machine was making all the right motions for us. That damn, wonderful machine.

Just as I was gathering my strength to throw her off and leap to my feet in indignation, I realized someone else had entered the room.

"Joy, damnit, move your head," someone said in a voice two octaves too high. She did, and Dr. Carlyle hit me between the eyes with something hard. Harder than my head, anyway. I went somewhere else for a while.

I can't move my arms. The fat one standing behind now gripping my elbows, my hands going numb. Run Jimmy! The ugly one leering, fumbling with his belt . . . Hold the little bastard . . . run . . . Jimmy . . . help me! . . . You kick me I'll wring your skinny neck. My right hand in my hip pocket, feeling the switchblade, cold, smooth . . . the button under my thumb . . . a metallic click, more felt than heard and I'm driving the knife backward, into a fleshy thigh . . . God! The screaming . . . him? . . . or me. . . .

I was waking up. I wasn't happy about it at the time, but

looking back, I suppose even that pain was better than the alternative. My head felt like something very angry was trying to gnaw its way out from behind my eyes. My hands were fastened behind my back. I was lying on a rough and uneven surface that kept moving in an erratic, no longer erotic motion. After a moment I realized I was on the floor in the back seat of a car, traveling at a high speed. My head was covered with what smelled like a dusty wool blanket, my legs folded up and cramped. All in all I was pretty miserable.

I must have moved or made a sound, because soon the blanket was removed, and after my eyes adjusted, I was looking up into the smiling face of Joy, my friendly nurse.

"Hello again, Mr. Jacobs. How you doin'?"

"Terrific. Thanks for asking."

"Aren't you supposed to say something like, 'Where am I?' "

"I think I know where I am. Where am I going?"

"I don't know. Some place Andrew uses, I guess."

"Joy, shut up. And keep him down on the floor. We're in traffic, and I don't want him trying to attract attention." The voice from the driver's seat sounded like the good Doctor.

"He looks funny. Like a raccoon. You blacked his eyes, Sugarbear." She giggled, and Sugarbear grunted.

"It should have killed him. I hit him hard enough."

"Well, you'll have another chance soon, and you damn well better get it done this time." This was a different voice, coming from the front seat. A man's voice. Loud, deep, with a quality that seemed to say, "Listen to me, I know what I'm talking about." I thought hard, and deduced it must be the lawyer, Harlan Ridgeway.

"Shove it, Harlan." Right again. I was starting to get the

hang of this detective stuff.

"You shove it, you prick. I wouldn't be in this mess if you hadn't talked me into it. I was doing all right with my practice. I never should have listened to you. 'It'll be easy, Harlan. Think of all that money, Harlan. No one will ever know.' All the time showing off your big house, and your cars, and that cheap piece of ass you married. Married, for God's sake. Two years ago you could have bought her for a hundred dollars."

Joy smiled down at me, sweetly, and said, "That would be me they're talking about. But he's wrong, honey. No one could have had me for a hundred bucks. I was top of the line." She slipped her right shoe off and began to rub her foot against my bare chest while she fingered a button on her blouse. "And I do mean, top of the line."

"Listen to that. Is that any way for your wife to talk? You must be real proud."

"Shut up, Harlan. Just shut the fuck up! She's my wife and I love her."

"Why, thank you, Sugarbear. You're a darling."

"Goddamnit, Joy, you shut up too. I've got to think."

All of a sudden Ridgeway sounded more nervous than mad. "What's there to think about? We have our orders, Carlyle. You know what he'll do to us if we screw this up." And I was wondering just who "he" was. So I asked Joy.

"Who are they talking about now?"

"Harlan is afraid of Andrew. Hell, everybody is afraid of Andrew, except me. I know how to handle him. I can handle any man."

"I'll bet you . . ."

"Joy. Keep your mouth shut, I mean it."

"Why, Sugarbear, what's come over you? You certainly never asked me to shut my mouth before."

The bickering went on, and on. I tuned them out, more interested in my own problems than theirs. It was getting dark. At least I hoped it was getting dark, because it was getting hard for me to see Joy's pouting face. The car was traveling at a high, constant speed, and I knew we were on the highway—a highway leading to my final resting place, no doubt. The rope on my wrists was tight, my fingers numb. Nothing would give. As much as I wanted to kick someone, I couldn't straighten my legs. I did notice one promising thing. Lying on the seat next to my nurse, tucked in the corner, were my shirt, tie, and coat. I presume they brought my clothes along to be sure no evidence was left behind. I also presumed that, in the left inside coat pocket, rested my little automatic knife. Cold to the touch . . . smooth . . . sharp . . . and so near.

Before too long we slowed, then turned right onto a gravel road. A few minutes later the road became steep and rutted, seemingly almost more than the car, a new Lincoln, could handle. But we made it. Great.

It was completely dark outside, and after staring up into the dome light when the doors opened, I couldn't see a damn thing when they dragged me out and dropped me into the dirt. As the circulation returned to my legs, I realized my ankles were tied, too. Carlyle and Ridgeway stood near the front fender of the big sedan, arguing in whispers about something. Joy stood over me, combing her hair with her fingers. She wasn't very happy either, but she was a trooper.

"Damn, I hate the woods. Bugs, and spiders, and . . . things. They didn't have to drag me out here."

"Sorry to be so much trouble," I apologized.

"You don't mean that, I know, but you are trouble. Big trouble, for all of us. You're trying to spoil a good thing.

We were going to Europe this year, on a month-long tour. Now, I don't know." She was still pouting. "Damnit, I've never been to Europe."

"Well, I imagine the good doctor and your family attorney are over there now, working out something to solve all your problems. I sure won't be much trouble to them like this, with my hands and feet tied. Unless, of course, you would like to reconsider your part in this, and untie me. I would make sure the cops knew you saved my life. You could walk away scot-free."

"Free? With what? They'd make us give back all the money. I wouldn't have anything. And I'm not going back to . . . No sir. You made your own bed, now die in it." She giggled. "Hey, that's pretty good. You made your own bed, now die in it. I like that."

"Joy, honey, go inside and turn on a light. The key is over the door. There's a shotgun in the back bedroom. Bring it to me."

"What the hell are you doing in bedrooms out here? You and Andrew play with each other, or have you been keeping something on the side?"

"Just get the goddamn gun."

"Get your own damn gun. You're not going to make me an accessory."

"What the hell do you think you are now, you stupid . . . never mind. I'll get it myself."

My eyes had adjusted enough for me to see Carlyle climb three steps up onto a wooden porch. The large shadow behind him turned out to be a cabin. A lamp came on inside, throwing squares of light onto the gravel driveway. I could see Ridgeway's feet near the car, the rest of him hidden in shadow. I could make out the blade of a shovel, resting on the ground next to his feet. Well, now I knew what they had been arguing about. Who would dig my grave. Carlyle came back down the steps, carrying a pump 12-gauge.

"Let's drag him over to those trees behind the shed," he said. "The ground is soft there."

"I can walk, if you'd untie my feet."

"Yeah. You can run, too, smart-ass."

They had quite a time of it, trying to drag me by my feet, while carrying the shovel and the shotgun. I didn't help. Actually, I did everything I could to hinder them, including driving both feet into Carlyle's groin when he got too close trying to grab my ankles. He responded with the butt of the shotgun to my forehead, which did nothing for my headache.

I lost the struggle, of course, and we ended up in a grove of persimmon trees about thirty yards from the cabin. I was having some very bad thoughts about the two of them, but when Ridgeway called out instructions to Joy, I became almost fond of him.

"Joy, bring his clothes from the car. They go in on top of him. We can't have any little clues lying around now, can we?"

Joy, bless her heart, brought the clothes and tossed them down next to me. Where they would be handy when the hole was finished. I waited until she had turned away to watch the digging, and twisted around and over till the coat was behind me, close to my hands. I had to move slowly, because they had dropped me onto a pile of dried leaves, and every movement caused a loud rustling sound I couldn't hide. I could still move my fingers enough to fumble around, feeling for the pocket. The problem was, my fingers were growing more numb every minute, and I could barely feel the cloth.

Fortunately it was very dark under the trees. They had Joy hold a flashlight while they took turns digging, and even when she turned toward me every few minutes, I had enough warning to stop moving before the light hit me. I finally felt the knife through the cloth, but it was still several minutes before I could find the pocket opening. Then, when I had the switchblade in my hand, at first I couldn't tell which end was which, and I couldn't find the button. When I did finally get the damn . . . the wonderful little thing to open, I cut my hand several times before I was able to get the blade on the rope around my wrists. Then all I had to do was keep from bleeding to death before they got close enough for me to use the knife. On them.

They finished the hole in about fifteen minutes. I wasn't quite ready.

"That's not very deep. Shouldn't you make it deeper? You don't want some animal digging me up."

"Shut up. It's deep enough. Go ahead, Harlan. Do it."

"The hell you say. You do it. I've never even fired a gun before. I'd more than likely shoot myself. You're the great outdoors man, you do it."

"I fish, for God's sake. I've never killed anything except fish."

I decided to express my own opinions on the matter. "Look, guys, why don't we talk this over? I mean it's obvious neither one of you really wants to do this, and I for one would certainly like for you to reconsider your options." I didn't think there was a chance, but it was worth a try.

Carlyle whirled on me like a madman. "Damn you, shut up! This is your fault, anyway. If you had stayed out of it, we wouldn't be in this mess." He was almost in tears.

Joy spoke up, not really defending me, but simply correcting her Sugarbear. "It wasn't really him, you know. It was that damn Jimmy that started this whole thing. If he hadn't been so greedy, we'd still be just cruising along, making all that lovely money."

Carlyle turned on her. "You've got a lot of nerve, talking about someone else being greedy. Ever since we got married you've been after me to do more, make more, buy more . . . I'm damn sick of it. If I could get out of this without going to jail, damned if I wouldn't just walk away, give it all up."

"Could you give me up, darlin'?" She moved to lean heavily against Carlyle's arm, and when he pulled away from her, she almost fell.

"Right now I'd trade you for a bus ticket to Mexico." He turned toward me with the shotgun, his back to her. I could see her face, suddenly twisted and ugly with anger. She slammed the flashlight against the back of his head, knocking him forward. He tripped over my feet and fell full length on top of me. I flung my hands up to catch him, more in self defense than anything. The little knife, which only a moment before had cut through the rope around my wrists, was still clutched in my right hand. It pierced his left shoulder, just under the collar bone, and I felt the blade snap off. As I pushed him off of me, I found the barrel of the shotgun in my left hand, and even before Joy started screaming, I had the gun turned around and pointed at Ridgeway. As Joy rushed to help Carlyle, she dropped the flashlight, but it was still working, and in the dim reflected light I could see the shock on Ridgeway's face. I'm not sure which of us was more surprised. I know I was almost certainly the happiest.

"So, since I had control of the shotgun, I convinced Ridgeway to untie my ankles, and as soon as I could walk I put everyone back into the car, me and Carlyle in the back, and Ridgeway drove us to the nearest phone. The sheriff's deputy arrived before long, with an ambulance for Carlyle, and you know the rest."

Sweet grunted, not impressed. It wasn't really late, but I had started yawning about a half hour earlier. I was in my favorite chair, he was on the couch, and Sherry was next to him, pouring more coffee. Since everything happened out of his jurisdiction, my reporting to him was more of a favor than an obligation. He certainly had access to all the official reports, but he had wanted to hear it directly from me, and had agreed to stop by our home for a visit. I had been retelling events of the previous night, trying not to over-embellish, while at the same time leaving out some of the parts that made me look and feel foolish, and a couple of things Sherry didn't need to know about. I felt I looked foolish enough, with both my eyes black and blue, and bloodshot.

"No phone at the cabin?" Sweet questioned.

"What?"

"I wonder why there wasn't a phone at the cabin. You described it as a nice place. Maybe worth two hundred grand, you said. Not just a hunting cabin or a fishing shack. You'd think they would have a phone."

"Well . . . I suppose . . . I hadn't really thought." Why the hell hadn't I thought to look in the cabin for a phone?

"These days everyone uses cellular phones. They probably didn't need one at the cabin." Either Sherry was being practical, or she was trying to save me from still another embarrassment.

"Well, at least you came out of it all right this time." He couldn't keep from smiling as he glanced at my black eyes.

"No, he didn't. The doctor says he has a concussion."

Sherry was still angry because I had let myself get hurt again.

"He said a mild concussion, sweetheart. I'm just fine."

"He said you might have dizzy spells, and have trouble concentrating for a while. Not that that would be so different from normal," she sniffed.

"Sweet, who owns the cabin up there? Do they know yet?" I thought it best to change the subject, and that was something I had been wondering about.

"The Carlyles and Ridgeway aren't talking yet, though I am sure they will eventually. County Real Property records show the owner to be a corporation, something called MedCon."

"MedCon? I've heard of that somewhere. What is it?" I guess I really was having trouble concentrating.

"We don't know yet, but some people are looking into it."

"What about 'Andrew'?" I was hoping Sweet could fill in a few missing pieces.

"We don't know that, either. Not yet. Like I said, someone will eventually talk. Either Ridgeway or Joy Carlyle. I've requested an opportunity to question them myself. I'm still waiting for the go-ahead."

"I'd bet on Ridgeway." I could still hear the desperation in his voice as he complained to Carlyle. "He sounded like the weak link. You may have to offer him a deal. Joy would spill her guts for enough money, but I don't suppose she qualifies for any reward."

"Not likely, but stranger things have happened. This thing has turned into a real tangle for everyone, as far as jurisdiction is concerned. Foster was killed in Broken Arrow by Jay. You took out Jay here in Tulsa, and Loomis shot Holloway here. The Yates woman was killed in Oklahoma

City. We know Loomis killed her, but we took Loomis in Tulsa, and you were kidnapped here, but they carried you all the way out to Keystone Lake, and they were eventually arrested by Osage County authorities, who will have to turn them over to Tulsa. I get a headache just trying to keep track of the paperwork." For a moment, frustration showed on his face. "This whole thing started in my jurisdiction, and the longer it goes on the more I get pushed out of the picture." He sighed and shook his head. "Well, I'd better get back home. Thanks again for the coffee, Ms. Jacobs." He rose from the couch, pausing halfway up, bent forward slightly at the waist, in some parody of a bow toward Sherry.

"Not at all, Detective Sweet. You're welcome here anytime. You should bring your wife next time. We could have dinner, perhaps play some cards." Sherry followed him to the door. I stood also, but being a recovering, heroic invalid, I remained at my chair.

"I'm sure she'd like that very much, thank you. Take care of yourself, Jacobs. Goodnight, Ma'am."

Sherry locked the door behind him and began gathering up the coffee cups, carrying everything to the kitchen. I sat back down and tried to think everything through. Again.

Jimmy Jay shot me, and now he was dead. Loomis shot at me, and killed Chris Yates and Dennis Holloway, but now Loomis was dead. Carlyle and Ridgeway tried to kill me, with Joy's good wishes, and now all three of them were in custody. Carlyle was recovering from the stab wound, and all reports were that he would certainly mend in time for the trial, which, given the speed of justice in our courts today, could happen any time between next Tuesday and my retirement date.

Underhill Life and Casualty was off the hook for Holloway, unless his heirs pressed the matter, and nothing had been heard from Nelson Cook since, after no doubt reading about Holloway and Chris Yates, he apparently decided he would be healthier somewhere else. The cops were looking for him as a material witness, and maybe as an accessory, but I wasn't holding my breath. Besides, there was ample evidence that the claims were phony, set up by Carlyle and Ridgeway. And that was enough to satisfy J. W. Kellogg and Underhill Life and Casualty. So, what's left?

"Who the hell is Andrew?" I asked, unconsciously looking at Jackson, who was lying nearby, watching me closely. At the sound of my voice he growled softly, lurched to his feet, and ran into the kitchen to hide behind Sherry. He was no help.

Andrew, the guy Carlyle and Ridgeway took orders from. The man they were afraid of, and who Joy was so sure she could control. And who, obviously, controlled all of them instead. The last word was that all three of them were standing mute, not talking to anyone but their lawyers. That meant "Andrew" was still in control, wherever and whoever he might be.

Glancing at the clock I saw that it was just past 8:00 P.M. I grabbed the phone and called Tal's number.

"What?" He has absolutely no phone etiquette.

"Tal, it's Carl. I have another little job for you. I'm looking for a man, first name Andrew. Wait a minute. I guess that might be his last name. Check it both ways. He should have some connection with Carlyle and Ridgeway, and probably Jimmy Jay, too. And he probably hired Loomis, though I suppose either one of the other two could have. And while you're at it, see what you can find out about MedCon. I think you told me they owned most of Shannon Research. They also own a cabin up at Keystone.

loway, unless his heirs pressed the matter, and nothing had been heard from Nelson Cook since, after no doubt reading about Holloway and Chris Yates, he apparently decided he would be healthier somewhere else. The cops were looking for him as a material witness, and maybe as an accessory, but I wasn't holding my breath. Besides, there was ample evidence that the claims were phony, set up by Carlyle and Ridgeway. And that was enough to satisfy J. W. Kellogg and Underhill Life and Casualty. So, what's left?

"Who the hell is Andrew?" I asked, unconsciously looking at Jackson, who was lying nearby, watching me closely. At the sound of my voice he growled softly, lurched to his feet, and ran into the kitchen to hide behind Sherry. He was no help.

Andrew, the guy Carlyle and Ridgeway took orders from. The man they were afraid of, and who Joy was so sure she could control. And who, obviously, controlled all of them instead. The last word was that all three of them were standing mute, not talking to anyone but their lawyers. That meant "Andrew" was still in control, wherever and whoever he might be.

Glancing at the clock I saw that it was just past 8:00 P.M. I grabbed the phone and called Tal's number.

"What?" He has absolutely no phone etiquette.

"Tal, it's Carl. I have another little job for you. I'm looking for a man, first name Andrew. Wait a minute. I guess that might be his last name. Check it both ways. He should have some connection with Carlyle and Ridgeway, and probably Jimmy Jay, too. And he probably hired Loomis, though I suppose either one of the other two could have. And while you're at it, see what you can find out about MedCon. I think you told me they owned most of Shannon Research. They also own a cabin up at Keystone.

City. We know Loomis killed her, but we took Loomis in Tulsa, and you were kidnapped here, but they carried you all the way out to Keystone Lake, and they were eventually arrested by Osage County authorities, who will have to turn them over to Tulsa. I get a headache just trying to keep track of the paperwork." For a moment, frustration showed on his face. "This whole thing started in my jurisdiction, and the longer it goes on the more I get pushed out of the picture." He sighed and shook his head. "Well, I'd better get back home. Thanks again for the coffee, Ms. Jacobs." He rose from the couch, pausing halfway up, bent forward slightly at the waist, in some parody of a bow toward Sherry.

"Not at all, Detective Sweet. You're welcome here anytime. You should bring your wife next time. We could have dinner, perhaps play some cards." Sherry followed him to the door. I stood also, but being a recovering, heroic invalid, I remained at my chair.

"I'm sure she'd like that very much, thank you. Take care of yourself, Jacobs. Goodnight, Ma'am."

Sherry locked the door behind him and began gathering up the coffee cups, carrying everything to the kitchen. I sat back down and tried to think everything through. Again.

Jimmy Jay shot me, and now he was dead. Loomis shot at me, and killed Chris Yates and Dennis Holloway, but now Loomis was dead. Carlyle and Ridgeway tried to kill me, with Joy's good wishes, and now all three of them were in custody. Carlyle was recovering from the stab wound, and all reports were that he would certainly mend in time for the trial, which, given the speed of justice in our courts today, could happen any time between next Tuesday and my retirement date.

Underhill Life and Casualty was off the hook for Hol-

Nice place to visit, but I almost died there. The authorities are looking along these same lines, so you have a little competition. I'd appreciate it if you came up with the information first. Besides, they may not feel obliged to share their findings with me."

"I'm having dinner."

"Yeah? In bits and bytes, no doubt."

"What?"

"Never mind. Did you get all of that?"

"All of what?" He hung up on me. He does have a strange sense of humor.

CHAPTER ELEVEN

I had an appointment to see a doctor the following Wednesday afternoon, so he could check my head again for cracks, or something. They didn't find any, but by then my face looked like something an abstract artist would paint on a bad day. My forehead was still swollen where Carlyle had slugged me with the gun butt. Both eyes were still black and only partially open, and showed more red than white. I never have been very pretty, but after what Carlyle did to me I was a mess, though the doctor assured me, and Sherry, that there was no permanent damage.

Sherry took a day off from work and drove me because I still wasn't allowed to drive, and because she didn't trust me to tell her the truth about what the doctor said. On the way home I had to talk fast to convince her to stop by Tal's computer room/garage. It had been three days since I last talked with him, and I wasn't about to just sit around until he called me. I wanted information.

Sherry waited in the car while I walked slowly up the driveway to the side door of the garage and entered. Tal buzzed me in through the security lock, and while he was staring at my face I beat him to the punch. "Yeah, I know. I look terrible. As a matter of fact, I feel terrible too, and I don't want to talk about it. Okay?"

"Your eyes are green."

"They've always been green, Tal."

"No, I mean around the eyes. I've seen black eyes before, but your black eyes are turning green. Don't they hurt? They look really awful."

"You should see them from the inside. What have you got for me?"

"Everything." He smirked a self-satisfied little smirk as he said it.

"Everything? What is that, everything?"

"I have everything you need, Carl. As Sergeant Preston of the Northwest Mounties used to say, 'Well, King, this case is closed.' "

"Come on, give. What have you found . . . ? Wait a minute. Where in the hell did you ever hear about Sergeant Preston and his trusty dog King? That was ancient before you were born."

"I have an inquiring mind. I study things. Even old radio programs. Did you know you can buy them now, on cassette tapes? I have a library of . . ."

"Okay. Okay, that's great. Right now all I want to know is what you have found out. What have you pulled out of that magic box of yours?"

He picked up a file folder lying nearby and passed it to me. "It's all in there. I can summarize it for you if you like."

"I would like that very much, Tal."

"MedCon, as I told you before, owns over half interest in the CAT scan business. The rest is owned by a consortium of lawyers, chiropractors, medical doctors, even an anesthesiologist. MedCon also owns the cabin up at Keystone Lake, as you said."

"Okay, so who or what is MedCon? Tell me something I don't know."

"MedCon is owned by another company, which is a subsidiary of a corporation, which is run by a holding company, which is . . . well, it goes on and on, but what you are interested in is a name, right? The name of a real live person?"

"Yes, Tal, that would be very helpful. Have you got a name for me?"

"Sure. It's Andrew." He paused just long enough to be extremely irritating, then dropped the bombshell. "Andrew Baker."

"Andrew . . . Andy Baker? The insurance adjuster?"

"The one and only. From what I have found out, he works for Underhill Life and Casualty. Isn't that the same place you do so much work for, Carl?" He grinned, rubbing it in.

"That son-of-a-bitch. Of course. Who would be better at committing insurance fraud than an insurance adjuster? Or helping other people commit fraud? Especially if the policies were written by Underhill. He was the adjuster for the Holloway claim, and the Cook claim. He recommended settlement in both cases, but Kellogg over-ruled him and hired me to investigate them. I'll bet that pissed Baker off."

"I guess you could say that. He tried to have you killed," Tal reminded me.

"But . . . Jimmy shot at me even before I was working on the Holloway claim. That doesn't make sense."

"Carl, it makes sense if Baker knew you were going to be hired. Don't you suppose someone may have told him?"

"I guess so." I considered. "Sherry knew before I did, I guess Baker could have known as well. My God, he's probably been doing this for years."

"I found something else, Carl. Something that ties it all together."

"What?" I was still puzzled with the suddenness of Tal's findings. I felt like someone had just turned on a bright light and my eyes hadn't yet adjusted.

"Your friend, Jimmy Jay. He filed a large injury claim about eight months ago for a back injury. It was with a different insurance company, but Carlyle was his doctor, and Ridgeway was his attorney. He collected over fifteen thousand dollars from an auto accident."

"Come on, Tal, Jimmy never had even fifteen hundred dollars in his pocket his whole life, let alone fifteen thousand dollars. At least not until someone paid him ten thousand dollars to kill Foster. Believe me, if Jimmy had that kind of money . . . but of course. He wouldn't have, would he? Most of it went to his attorney, and his doctor. And probably a lot to his technical advisor, Andrew Baker."

Tal shook his head, puzzled. "Still, that doesn't seem like enough money to kill someone for."

"No, it doesn't, does it? Not to you or me. But I guess it looked like a lot more to Jimmy. Especially since he didn't get to keep much of the fifteen-thousand-dollar insurance claim." Another thought occurred to me. "And soon after that he took out a policy with Underhill, and then tried to file a claim on some imaginary items stolen from his apartment. He probably thought the first one worked so well he would pull another one, this time on his own, so that he could keep all the money for himself. If Sherry hadn't drawn that case, he may have gotten away with it."

"How do you suppose Baker felt when he found out Jay was moonlighting, filing claims on his own?" Tal asked.

"He would have been furious. Jimmy striking out on his own would endanger the master plan. That's what Joy meant when she said the whole mess they were in was Jimmy's fault, for being too greedy." I was suddenly full of answers and anxious to put them to work. "Thanks, Tal. You've made my day."

"My pleasure. Let me know how everything turns out," he called to my back as I headed for the door.

I brought Sherry up to date in the car on the way home.

Twice she had to pull over to the curb and stop while she tried to digest the idea that one of the men she worked with every day was a murderer. "I can't believe it. I mean, I can't stand the guy, he makes my skin crawl every time he touches me, but it would never occur to me that he could actually kill somebody."

"What do you mean, when he touches you? What the hell is he doing, touching you?"

"Oh, Carl, you know. Nothing serious, just a pat on the shoulder, or his hand on my arm when he was talking to me. He wasn't making a pass, or anything. I just thought he was a touchy-sort-of guy. A lot of you are, you know." She turned away from me to look over her shoulder and check for traffic before pulling away from the curb, but I thought I saw a twitch of a smile at the corner of her mouth.

At the next intersection she turned left, instead of right toward our house. "Where are you going?" I asked.

"I'm going to the police station, where do you think," she announced, rather incredulously. "We've got to report this, and have them pick up Andy."

"Sherry, please. Just turn around and go home. I'm going to call Sweet and let him handle it. I owe it to him. He's been up front with me—sort of—and he deserves a chance to break the case."

She argued a little, pointing out that the longer Baker was loose, the more time he had to get to me, but I finally convinced her that a couple of hours wouldn't make that much difference. Yeah, right.

It was 2:00 P.M. when we got home, and I started trying to reach Sweet right away, but he wasn't available, and no one at the Broken Arrow PD would give me a clue. They just kept saying they would pass on my request for Sweet to call me back. I insisted it was urgent, but apparently they had other priorities. It was after 5:00 P.M. before Sweet called. "Sorry, Jacobs, but I've been tied up. What can I do for you?"

"It's what I can do for you, my friend. How would you like to tie up the loose ends of the Foster murder and put away the man who hired Jimmy Jay and Percival Loomis?"

Sherry was hovering over my shoulder and immediately asked, "Who is Percival Loomis?"

"Later, sweetheart. Well, Sweet, have I got your attention?"

"You have. What crystal ball did you use?"

"No crystal ball, simply superior detective work. Have you got a pencil? You may want to write this down."

"Get on with it, Jacobs."

"As soon as possible you will want to pick up one Andrew Baker. Just a minute. Sherry, do you know Baker's address?"

"No I don't. Who is Percival Loomis?"

Sweet interrupted just as I was shaking my head at her. "Don't bother, Jacobs. Baker lives in a condominium on South 73rd East Avenue. But he's not home right now."

After a very long pause, while I tried to figure out what the hell was happening, I managed to ask, "How do you know that?"

"Because I'm sitting in front of his place right now, along with two squad cars of uniformed officers, and a warrant for Baker's arrest as a material witness in a murder investigation."

"How . . . ?"

"I guess my superior detective work is a little better than your superior detective work. Or at least a few hours faster. We've been here since noon, but he hasn't shown. He's not at the office, either. Left for lunch and hasn't been back."

"Terrific."

"What's terrific?" Sherry wanted to know. "And who the hell is Percival Loomis?"

Late Wednesday evening, after the girls were in bed, Sweet stopped by the house to explain. "I'm not sure what happened. Before we went to his place we stopped at Underhill, and they said he had just left for lunch. When we got to the condo he wasn't there, so we set up down the street to wait for him to show. We think he may have stopped off somewhere along the way, then when he finally got home he spotted us waiting for him and took off. If he knew how little we really had on him, he would have stayed to bluff it out."

"What do you mean, how little we have? We know he's back of everything. Jimmy, Loomis, the Yates girl—everything." Needless to say, I was pretty pissed that Baker had got away.

"Come on, Jacobs, knowing it and proving it are two different things. Right now we may be able to charge Baker with insurance fraud, or conspiracy to commit insurance fraud, but beyond that it's all speculation. We can't connect him to Loomis at all. We can barely connect the Blue Jay to the Foster killing. We know Loomis killed Holloway and the Yates girl, but we can't prove Baker ordered it."

Sherry was an interested party and had plenty of questions of her own. "What do you have on Andy, other than the fact that he owns part of the CAT scan outfit, Shannon Research?"

"That's about it. We're still looking into it, and we're bound to come up with a lot of circumstantial evidence of fraud, and maybe even get him on some sort of racketeering charges, but that's still to come. In the meantime, Baker could be doing exactly what he told your boss, Kellogg,

Friends and Other Perishables

when he phoned in this afternoon—taking some time off for personal reasons."

"That leaves us with Carlyle and Ridgeway. And Joy, of course. We may be able to get them to finger Baker," I pointed out, with little conviction.

"Not likely," Sweet growled. "I hear they're standing mute, at the suggestion of their attorney, Alfred Binger."

"Binger," Sherry spat out. "The best damn criminal attorney in the state. At least we know where they'll be spending a lot of the money they've been scamming. Hell, they may even get off. If anyone can save them, Binger can."

"Honey, how can he get them off? I'm a witness. If nothing else I can testify all three of them conspired to kidnap and kill me. There's just no way they can avoid going to prison after I testify."

"If you testify," corrected Sweet.

"If? Oh, yeah. But with them in jail and Baker on the run, who's going to stop me?"

Sherry nodded, and looked to Sweet for an answer we were both hoping he couldn't come up with.

"Well, first of all, they're not in jail—they made bail. Two hundred and fifty thousand dollars, each. And secondly, we don't know that Baker has run all that far. He may still be in town, or he may leave for a while then come back to finish his chores after things have cooled off. Either way, you should be careful for a while. Don't you think?"

"No, he hasn't been spending much time thinking lately," Sherry answered for me. "He just bulls his way around, convinced that he's bulletproof, or something."

"If I hadn't been thinking, and finding out things the way a good investigator is supposed to do, we wouldn't be in this mess, would we? And now you expect me to think some more. You're never satisfied. I have a headache. Stop picking on me."

"Yes, dear. Detective Sweet, may I get you some more coffee?"

"No, thank you. I have to go. Jacobs, get some sleep. You don't look too good."

We walked Sweet to the door and stood on the porch watching him drive away. The night air was finally cold and crisp, the way October air is supposed to be, and Sherry moved closer to me, indicating an arm around her shoulders would be welcome.

The sky was clear, the stars bright, and the moon full. Romance was in the air, and in Sherry's' voice as she said, softly, "Darling?"

"Yes, sweetheart?"

"Who is Percival Loomis?"

I reluctantly explained to her that the vicious hired gun, Lou Giannetti, killer of Dennis Holloway, and sweet little Chris Yates, and the man who shot her very own beloved husband, was known by several names, among them, Percival Loomis. I then swept her up in my arms and carried her upstairs for a most passionate interlude, marred only by the occasional giggle, and the name "Percy" murmured softly against my neck.

The next day I insisted that we alter our routine. Instead of Sherry dropping the girls off at their grandparents and going to work, as she usually does, I went along. I even drove, against Sherry's wishes. My head had stopped throbbing, and my eyes were almost completely open. Besides, the doctor had pronounced me homely but fit only the day before. And I wasn't about to let Sherry go to work alone, to find Baker sitting at his desk as though nothing had happened.

Friends and Other Perishables

When we arrived at Underhill, the first thing I did was make sure Baker hadn't shown up for work that morning. The receptionist said he hadn't, adding that he hadn't called, either. After pecking me on the cheek, even though she knows that public displays of affection embarrass me, Sherry went to her desk to start her day. I decided to stop in and visit with Mr. Kellogg and maybe dig up some more information about Baker.

His secretary, Donna, told me Kellogg had a visitor, but she announced me anyway, and I was surprised when I was invited to go on in. Mr. Kellogg was standing just inside the door, waiting to shake my hand the moment I entered, something he had done perhaps three times in eleven years. He didn't like personal contact with anyone, so I was very surprised, until I recognized the visitor. The tall, slender man with gray hair, yellow tie, black suit, and gold-handled ebony walking stick was Cornelius V. Latham, one of the most powerful men ever to walk the halls of the White House without ever having held public office. He was to politics what the M.I.T. think-tank was to the sciences. He had been whispering into the ears of world leaders for more than forty years. He advised them, tutored them, praised, and scolded them as needed. The one thing he didn't do was vote. The media was always after him to endorse this candidate, or that candidate, but he never committed himself, at least publicly, to any one individual. Only to ideas and methods. He was probably the only man in Washington D.C. who was equally trusted, feared, and courted by members of all parties.

"Come in, Carl. There's someone here who has been wanting to meet you. Mr. Latham, this is the young man I mentioned to you, Carl Jacobs. Carl, I'd like to introduce Mr. Cornelius Latham." Kellogg was watching me closely to be sure I was properly in awe of his visitor.

"Mr. Latham, of course. This is an honor, Sir." So, what the hell are you supposed to say when you meet a living legend?

"Actually, Mr. Jacobs, I believe I am the one who should feel honored. You see, I knew your father, years ago. He was someone I deeply respected, as did everyone in Washington." His grip was firm, but he held on a little too long, and seemed to be examining my face for something—weakness or strength, I wasn't sure. Kellogg stood silent nearby, watching our exchange closely, like a fan at a tennis match.

"You knew my father? I had no idea he got around that much. He traveled a lot when I was young, but I always assumed it was mostly to the state capitol. I never dreamed he was known in Washington." This was not the first time I had been greeted warmly by strangers who had known my father, and who somehow expected to find him in me.

"Oh yes," Latham said with a smile, "you might say he got around. In fact, he spent much of his time in Europe, and the Middle East. Indeed, he got around." His expression changed, suddenly. "I was terribly sorry to hear of his passing. I believe the papers said natural causes?" he inquired, watching me closely.

Now, what the hell is this all about? This is twice someone has asked if my father died of natural causes.

"Yes, Sir. Natural causes. That's what his physician said. He was in his fifties."

"Mmmm. Well, I suppose we all have to answer the call eventually. Still, such a loss . . . You have my deepest sympathies."

"Thank you."

Kellogg cleared his throat at the first pause, and said, "Mr. Latham is interested in what progress you've made on this fraud investigation you're working."

"Oh? I'm surprised you even know about it."

"Well, I didn't until a few minutes ago. James told me about it because recently I have been working with a few of the larger, nationwide insurance carriers to see what might be done to curb the increasing burden of insurance fraud which we have to deal with. As I'm sure you know, it is costing the nation an average of ten billion dollars each year. We could do a lot with that kind of money, if we were able to channel it in other directions."

"Yes, I suppose so," I agreed, wondering exactly what channels he had in mind.

He grew silent for a moment, his eyes aimed at me, but obviously seeing something else, in a future his mind was busily conceiving. Suddenly he blinked and dropped back into the present.

"Well, again my condolences for the loss of your father."

"Thank you. You're very kind. Of course, it was seventeen years ago."

"My, my, seventeen years. I would have thought more like seven. I must be getting old, for time to pass so quickly." He turned suddenly to Kellogg. "Speaking of time, I really have to be going, James. Thank you so much for your help. I'll let you know how it goes. Mr. Jacobs, again it's been a pleasure meeting you. Your father was a fine man. His hard work and dedication to an ideal helped make this country the proud nation it is today. Be sure your children know the kind of man their grandfather was."

"Well, Sir, I'm beginning to wonder if I knew the kind of man he was. I mean, he was a wonderful father, but as for his work... I'm afraid he didn't talk about it very much."

"Really? That's a shame." Latham studied his feet for a moment, then fished into a coat pocket and handed me a business card. "Well, Carl, if you're ever in D.C. you come and see me. Maybe we can talk about old times. But I have to run. Good-bye, James. Mr. Jacobs." He left quickly, but took time to pull the door closed.

Kellogg and I stood there for a moment, in silence. Then, I had to ask, "What the hell was that all about?"

"I really don't know. I happened to mention your name this morning, just in passing conversation, and after he asked a few questions about you, he told me he had known your father, and would like to meet you if you were going to be available. I didn't want to bother you with it, but I suppose it's just as well you stopped in today."

"So, what was Cornelius Latham doing here, anyway? Is he renewing his health insurance or something?"

Kellogg turned away and retreated behind his desk without answering. When he was settled into his leather chair, he looked up and asked, "What can I do for you, Jacobs?"

That let me know where I stood. I decided that, while now was not the time, someday I was going to have to investigate my own father, just to make sure I knew who he really was.

"Nothing, really. I just brought Sherry to work, and I wanted to make sure Baker wasn't going to be here."

"He isn't. We haven't heard from him. Anything else?" he asked, starting to shuffle through papers on his desk.

"No, I suppose not. I'll leave. Wouldn't want to get in the way. I'll be in the bullpen talking to Sherry for a few minutes, if you need me for anything." I left the office before he said anything else and before I said anything that might cost me my best client. I found Sherry in her office and took out my frustrations on her. She didn't appreciate it.

Friends and Other Perishables

Before I left Sherry's office, having once again determined Baker was not on the premises, I was invited by Mr. Kellogg, probably his way of making up for my earlier abrupt dismissal, to attend a meeting of company employees, all eighteen of them, during which he explained the situation concerning the absent Mr. Baker. He was careful not to make blatant accusations, and simply reported what the police had told him. He left the impression it was all speculation, but he made it clear that anyone who had knowledge of Baker's activities or whereabouts should pass that information to the authorities. Then, after pumping me for all the details, Kellogg ordered Sherry and Barbara, the other adjuster, to review Baker's files. I hadn't realized it before, but Baker had been with the company only three years. For eight years prior to joining Underhill as an adjuster, according to his resume, he had worked at four other agencies in the same capacity. Obviously, he knew a good thing when he saw it, and I had no doubt he had been pulling the same scam for years. Kellogg, out of a sense of professional courtesy, had already been in contact with the other insurance companies, advising them of the situation and suggesting they might want to review Baker's records.

I left Underhill at 10:00 A.M., explaining to Sherry that I had a hundred things to take care of, and promising her I would pick her up after work. Downstairs, instead of running off to take care of those hundred things, I sat in the station wagon trying to think of even one thing which would prove useful. The best I could come up with was to drive to Broken Arrow and visit with Sweet, hoping he had some news about Baker.

"I don't know where the hell he is, Carl. If I did, I would go pick him up."

We were sitting at Sweet's desk, speaking in low tones to

avoid being heard by three or four other officers, of various ranks, scattered around the large room. Sweet didn't want anyone to know how he had been keeping me informed of their progress. After all, I was an outsider.

"Sweet, I don't expect you to work miracles, but you've got to know how important it is to me that this guy is found and locked up right away."

"I know. Believe me, it's important to me, too. I need this bust, and if I can get him before some other jurisdiction hauls him in, it will go well for me upstairs." He shook his head. "He just didn't leave any trail. We'll find him, eventually, but it's not going to be easy."

He was making me feel worse instead of better, so I left and went home. I spent the afternoon calling all of my contacts and informants, letting them know that there would be a bonus for anyone who could come up with a lead to Baker. They were sympathetic, but less than helpful. Baker had simply dropped out of sight. It went on like that for days—then weeks—and on through the holidays.

CHAPTER TWELVE

For the most part we led normal lives, pretending nothing was bothering us, trying not to jump when the phone rang, or when someone came to the front door. I suppose I did get in a little more practice than usual at the local indoor pistol range, and Bobby, the owner, was pleased with my improved scores. And as soon as my wounds were healed enough not to split open from exertion, I started going back to the gym to work out, trying to awaken muscles that hadn't been used in quite a while. My trainer wasn't quite as pleased with my progress, but I could still handle the weights up to a point, and I didn't embarrass myself. Much.

I got a few calls from informants offering leads on hot hospital equipment, but in every case they turned out to be mistaken, totally false, or having to do with drugs. No one had any information about wheelchairs or iron lungs. I did manage to make a few more friends with the local authorities by passing along the information I came up with, but had nothing that would help Annabelle, or Tal either. Annabelle called several times to find out if I had anything for her, and to tell me things were still disappearing. The list had grown considerably. She wasn't happy, and neither were the hospital board members. Time passed.

Sherry and I spent Halloween night walking the neighborhood a few paces behind the girls, as they went from house to house gathering their loot. Under my leather jacket I was wearing my .45 automatic in a shoulder holster. That was the first Halloween I had ever felt it was necessary to go "trick or treating" with a gun. Later that evening we carefully went through all of the candy, looking for anything suspicious, such as needles or razor blades. We live in a nice, middle class neighborhood, full of very nice people, but you just don't take chances with your children's safety. In fact, to be absolutely sure it was safe, I had to eat quite a lot of it myself, sacrificing my own health for the sake of my girls.

We spent the first half of Thanksgiving together as a family. Sherry cooked the obligatory turkey, as well as a small ham, along with all the trimmings. I tried my hand at baking pies, turning out a sad-looking, but edible chocolate cream and a rather remarkable deep dish pecan, then proceeded to eat more than my share of both. After dinner had settled and we had the kitchen more or less back to normal, Sherry and the girls left to spend the evening with the in-laws and assorted relatives. As I said before, Sherry's parents and I don't get along, and we avoid each other at every opportunity. On previous holidays I often felt a little guilty about it, but when Sherry told me she didn't have to make up any excuse for me, because her parents never asked where I was, I decided to accept the situation, and from that time on watched football games, alone, with a clear conscience.

It wasn't all holidays and eating, of course. I went back to work as soon as my face had turned a normal color and my eyes focused properly.

Finally, a week after Thanksgiving I got a good tip from one of my informants about the stolen hospital equipment. Of course it came at 2:00 one Thursday morning, while Sherry and I were both sound asleep. The phone in the bedroom is on my side, but I never seem to wake up enough to realize what all the racket is, until Sherry crawls across my inert body to answer it. In twelve years of marriage she has never gotten a call in the middle of the night. They have all been for me, and she keeps reminding me of it.

"Carl, it's for you. Naturally."

"Hunnnggmm?"

"The phone. It's for you. Wake up."

"No, thanks, I'm not hungry."

"CARL, DAMNIT, WAKE UP!"

"What? Okay, okay. Yes? Hello?"

"Jacobs, it's me. I told you I'd call when I had something."

"Who? Who is it?"

"It's me, Danny. I said I'd call you when I had something, and I got something, so I'm calling."

"What the hell have you got, insomnia?"

"No, Jacobs, I mean about the medical stuff. I think I found it."

"Where?" I asked, finally coming out of it.

"Near as I can tell, it's in a warehouse out at the port. Port of Catoosa. You know, where they load the barges to haul stuff down river."

"I know what a port is. Which one?"

"Like I said, the Port of Catoosa."

"Which warehouse, you moron?"

"That's no way to talk to me, Mr. Jacobs. After all, I'm just trying to help," he whined.

"I'm sorry, Danny. I just woke up. I apologize. Now, which warehouse?"

"Anderson Freight and Storage. The way I hear it, this pile of medical stuff is in a cubicle out there waiting to be shipped off to somewhere in South America. I got a cousin whose wife's brother drives a fork lift there. He says the pile gets bigger every month or so, and as soon as there's enough to fill one of those shipping container things, off it goes."

"What sort of stuff does your cousin's wife's brother say is in this pile? Any sign of an iron lung, or a dialysis machine?"

"Hell, he wouldn't know a dialysis from a dishwasher, but he did say he saw what looked like the outline of a wheelchair under a canvas tarp. You was looking for a wheelchair, wasn't you?"

"Yeah. Sounds good, Danny. Thanks. I'll take care of you next time I see you."

"No hurry, Mr. Jacobs. I know you're good for it. Just don't go getting shot, okay? I hear someone's been trying to cancel your ticket."

"Yeah. Keep a good thought, Danny."

"You too. Night."

I hung the phone up and lay back, staring up in the dark, trying to talk myself into just going back to sleep. It was wasted effort.

"Sherry, you still awake?"

"Hunnnggmm?"

"I have to go out. I'm sorry, but it's important."

"Mmm."

"I'll probably be working with a tall redheaded sexpot who used to be crazy about me. Is that okay with you?"

"Mm . . . I will, Mom. Night."

"Good night, sweetheart. I love you too."

"Phbbbksssss."

I grabbed some underwear and socks from a dresser drawer, and dressed inside the closet, pulling on a black pair of slacks and a black long-sleeved shirt. If I was going to go sneaking around a warehouse, I should be dressed appropriately. I added the little Smith & Wesson .38 to my attire, snapped into a strong-side belt holster, and covered everything up with my favorite black cardigan sweater, which had two buttons missing.

Downstairs I called the Riverside Hospital Security office. Annabelle wasn't there, of course. The guard wouldn't give me her home number, but when I convinced him it was important, and that it had to do with the missing hospital equipment, he said he could get a message to her. I told him to have her meet me in the parking lot of a convenience store just outside the main gate into the Port of Catoosa industrial complex.

It was after 3:00 A.M. before I got there, and I sat in the van drinking very old convenience store coffee waiting for Annabelle to show up. I took it for granted she would decide to join me. While I waited I tried to figure out why I hadn't just passed the information along to her, and gone back to sleep.

The Port of Catoosa industrial complex covers about two square miles of land situated next to the man-made waterway that flows into a series of rivers, lakes, locks, and dams, allowing inexpensive shipping of goods all the way to and from the Gulf of Mexico. I have no idea how much freight is shipped out of the state, destined for countries all over the world, stacked on barges which are pushed along by powerful little tugboats. Most of the stuff going out is probably grain and petroleum products. A lot of stuff coming in is probably raw materials and chemical products, like fertilizer. I know the complex is quite extensive and includes all sorts of manufacturing. I also knew there were a lot of highly sensitive areas within the complex, guarded by well trained and well equipped security outfits. Gaining unauthorized access to a warehouse in the middle of the night wasn't going to be easy.

I was about to talk myself out of it when Annabelle arrived, driving a beat-up old Ford pickup. I flashed my headlights at her and she parked a few slots away. She left the truck and nodded toward my van as she entered the convenience store. A few minutes later she came out and joined me, carrying her own cup of coffee. She wasn't in uniform. She had chosen an outfit similar to mine, with black pants and a black sweater, topped with a dark blue windbreaker, but I could see a bulge on her right hip where I didn't remember a bulge before, and I guessed she was wearing the 9mm automatic. She grunted a little as she climbed into my van.

"Sorry about the delay, C.J., but I had to make a head stop. Also, I needed this coffee. Thanks for the call. What have you got?"

"An informant of mine says he was told there is a pile of medical 'stuff' in a cubicle in a warehouse out here, Anderson Freight and Storage. He didn't have many details, and I understand some of the stuff is covered up with a tarp, but it sounded worth following up on. He thinks it's due to be shipped out any day now, to South America."

"I suppose that makes sense. That would explain why they didn't steal any drugs. Smuggling drugs into South America would be like shipping snow cones to Alaska. But of course, you don't have enough to interest the police, so you decided we should go in and see for ourselves. At 3:00 in the morning."

"I thought maybe you would want to go in. I could sit outside and honk the horn when the sheriff shows up."

"Yeah, right. Okay, Carl, I'm game. Let's do it."

I started up the van and drove toward the entrance to the complex just a short distance away. The guard shack wasn't occupied. I had been out there a hundred times for various reasons, and I had never seen a guard in the shack at the gate. I wasn't even sure why they had built it in the first place.

There were enough companies in the complex working all three shifts to provide some traffic in and out, so we weren't too conspicuous going in. We found the warehouse about half a mile from the gate, on the north side. I switched off my headlights and coasted to a stop in the parking lot near a couple of Dumpsters. We sat in the van for a while, just watching.

It was a two-story sheet metal building, probably 25,000 square feet. The entire east end of the building was one long loading dock, with bays and large overhead doors for maybe ten trucks at a time. There were security lights on all four sides of the building, and I counted three vehicles in the parking lot, but we couldn't see any lights through the large frosted glass windows. There was bound to be at least one guard inside, and probably a security company car patrolling the area.

"What do you say, Juicy Fruit? You in the mood for a little excitement?"

"Sure, but why don't we go in and look around first? We can get to the exciting part later." She pulled a small pair of binoculars out of her coat pocket and began studying the building. "If we leave the van here we can work our way along the fence to the west end, around back. There's a door at the corner, and the nearest light is probably twenty yards away. If we can get through there without being spotted, we'll have access to the rest of the building."

"Sounds okay. I imagine the guard room is toward the front, in the northeast corner over there, with the rest of the offices. Of course, the guard should be making rounds occasionally, but on the other hand, he may spend half his time sleeping. You know how those security people are."

"I know they're just poor slobs trying to make a living. We don't hurt anyone, no matter what. Right?" She wasn't asking, she was telling.

"I wasn't planning on shooting anyone tonight, Belle."

"Then I guess that must be a flask tucked in your belt. About a .38 caliber flask, I'd say."

"I just grabbed it out of habit. People have been shooting at me lately, and I'm not very good at chucking rocks. Besides, looks like you've got a bump, too. I don't suppose that's your flask?"

"No, I carry my flask in my hip pocket." She lifted one hip off the seat and pulled out a half-pint size brass colored flask, twisted the top open, and passed it to me. I sniffed, and decided it was probably bourbon. After a couple of swallows, I wasn't quite sure.

"What the hell is that stuff? You make it yourself?" My throat was burning and my eyes watered, but as the warmth spread into my stomach, I felt the knots in my shoulders start to loosen.

"No, I didn't make it myself, wise ass. That's the same stuff we used to drink when we were in high school." She took a stiff belt from the flask without making a face. "Remember, we used to buy it from Ray Baxter, for ten dollars a fifth? He bought it by the case in Missouri, probably for about three bucks, and bootlegged it to his friends. The son-of-a-bitch put himself through college with what he made off of us. I got so used to it back then, I still drink it today. Makes me all sentimental, and teary-eyed, just thinking about it. Want another shot?"

"No thanks, my eyes are teary enough." I did remember buying bootleg bourbon and vodka from Ray, back when the state was still dry. Funny, as I recalled, the stuff tasted better back then.

"No shooting, Carl. Okay? This guy in there is just some poor slob who can't hold down a real job. I've got my automatic with me, of course, but I'm not planning to use it." She paused. "In fact . . ." She reached under her windbreaker and pulled out the 9mm, then slid it under the passenger seat, out of sight. After a minute's hesitation, I drew my .38 and did the same.

We slipped out of the van, closing the doors quietly, and crept along the chain link fence, avoiding the patches of light cast by the occasional light pole in the parking lot. At the rear of the building we found the walk-through door locked, of course. The door was in the shadow of a large pile of wooden pallets stacked nearby. I pulled a pencil flashlight from my shirt pocket and examined the lock, then started working on it with a set of picks I had remembered to bring along. After about three minutes, the lock turned, and I pushed the door open.

"I'm impressed," Annabelle whispered. "Your hands used to shake so much, it took you longer than that to remove my bra."

"I don't get that excited about locked doors," I whispered back, and treasured visions of a young, bare-breasted Annabelle flashed through my memory. Concentrate, I told myself, and took a cautious look around.

We were in a cavernous room, the main storage room of the warehouse. What little light there was came from a few low-wattage light bulbs around the perimeter, high up on the walls. I could see that much of the interior was divided up into compartments, cubicles, formed by chain link fencing, ranging in size from maybe a hundred to five hundred square feet. Some of the cubicles had two levels, and some were full of boxes and containers stacked almost all the way to the high ceiling.

"Damn," Annabelle muttered, "this will take all night."

We moved further into the room, turning down an aisle between two rows of fenced-in storage compartments. I flashed the little pen light into each one. Some of the contents were readily identifiable, some were not. There were crates of machinery of various kinds, boxes of toilet paper, sacks of wheat, and fifty-five-gallon drums of stuff labeled "Flammable." Some piles were covered with canvas tarps. None of the cubicles had doors, so the contents were easily accessible, but it was going to take time and a hell-of-a-lot of luck to find what we were looking for.

I jumped a couple of feet straight up when Annabelle reached out and grabbed me by the arm. "Shhh. What's that noise?"

I stopped breathing and listened. There was a slight, rhythmic, clicking sound coming from somewhere ahead of us. I couldn't identify it at first, but I could tell it was getting louder—or closer. I tilted my head from side to side, trying to analyze the sound. Either Annabelle's eyes were better than mine, or else she guessed what the sound was before I could.

"Oh my God," she whispered. "Don't move."

Suddenly appearing out of the darkness, a large Doberman, toenails clicking on the concrete floor, trotted into view. At a distance of about twenty feet, he stopped, sat, and stared at us, tilting his head from side to side, much as I had just been doing. He didn't bark, or growl, or whine. He didn't make a sound. Those kind scare me the most.

"I don't suppose you have another pistol on you by any chance," I whispered out of the corner of my mouth at Annabelle.

Friends and Other Perishables

"Afraid not," she answered. "You?"

"No. Does he look hungry to you?"

"All Dobermans look hungry to me. We could turn around and run back to the door."

"You can't outrun a Doberman."

"I don't have to outrun him, I just have to outrun you."

"That's an old joke, and in damn poor taste," I whispered, remembering that when we were younger she always could outrun me.

"If you don't move, he won't eat you," said a voice from the darkness behind us. "Are you armed?" He was calm, and in complete control of the situation. My opinion of security guards was improving.

"No, Sir, we are not," Annabelle answered for us. "We meant no harm. We just wanted to look around."

The guard's footsteps echoed around us as he moved closer, then stepped in front of us to look closely at Annabelle. "Ms. Hicks? Is that you?"

"Yes, it is. And you're . . . Jason, right? Jason Pollard?"

"That's right. You remember me, huh?"

"Sure, I remember you, Jason. You were one of my best employees. I was sorry to see you go. So, you came to work out here, huh?"

"Yeah. The pay's a little better, but the working conditions aren't as nice. I kind of miss the hospital now and then. Especially the nurses."

"Excuse me?" I interrupted.

"Oh, sorry. Jason, this is a friend of mine, Carl Jacobs. He's a Private Investigator."

"No kidding? A private eye. Damn, that's what I wanted to do. How would I go about getting my license, Mr. . . . Jacobs, is it?"

"That's right. Say, could you tell your friend there everything's all right? He keeps looking at me and drooling."

"What? Oh, sure. Okay, Hitler, it's all over. Recall. Recall." The Doberman rose to his feet and started off toward the front of the building. He glanced back at me with what I thought was a look of disappointment.

The security guard was trying to find a balance between looking intimidating, and showing deference to Annabelle, someone he obviously admired. He held his right hand very still, close to the butt of the revolver he carried in a full police rig, strong side thumb snap holster, speed loaders readily available also on the strong side, with a six-cell metal-bodied Maglite held ready in his left hand. "Ms. Hicks, what are you doing in here? This is private property, and no one is allowed in here after business hours. You're putting me in a bad position."

"I know, Jason, and I'm sorry." She really did sound sorry. "Jason, we've had a problem at the hospital since you left. Someone has been stealing things, like an iron lung, and a kidney dialysis machine, as well a lot of small stuff. Mr. Jacobs here has been working the case for us, and he has information that some of the stolen goods are being stored here, in this warehouse. That's why we're here. We just wanted to look around, to see if his information was true, before we went to the police."

"Stolen? From the hospital? Damn, who would steal an iron lung? Somebody might need something like that, to keep on living." He suddenly thought of something else. "Why, you don't think I had anything to do with that, do you, Ms. Hicks?" He was very upset at the idea that Annabelle would suspect him of anything illegal.

"Of course not, Jason. I know you better than that. Besides, I didn't even know you worked here, until a moment ago. We weren't checking up on you, we were just looking for the stolen goods. The stuff is supposed to be in one of these cubicles."

"Which one?" he asked, looking around.

"We don't know, Jason," she said, patiently.

"Well, who stored it here?"

"We don't know that, either," I spoke up. "We don't even know for sure the stuff is here. One of my informants gave me the tip, but he might have been wrong."

He looked at me with new respect. "Wow! An informant. You must really know your business, Mr. Jacobs."

"Well, I've been doing it for a long time, Jason." I paused, then added, in a conspiratorial voice, "Say, Jason, do you suppose we could look around a little, before it gets too late?"

"Well . . . I suppose . . . I guess if Ms. Hicks vouches for you, it's okay. Hang on a minute." He hurried off.

I turned to a smiling Annabelle. "Who, might I ask, is going to vouch for you?"

"The kid has a crush on me. I can do no wrong. Hell, if I had known he worked here we could have just knocked on the door and asked for a tour." She smiled again. "He's actually a pretty good security guard, one of the best I ever trained."

"Sure. He must be all of twenty-two years old."

"The only thing wrong with youth is that you and I don't have our share anymore," she said philosophically. Suddenly the room was flooded with light, as Jason threw a switch somewhere. He came trotting back to us.

"That should help. If you can tell me what you're looking for, we could split up and save some time."

Annabelle described the stuff to him and we each took a different aisle. About ten minutes passed before I heard her calling from the far end of the room. By the time I got there, she and the kid had the tarp removed from the stack and were sorting through it. Sure enough, off to one side was a battery-powered wheelchair I recognized as Tal's.

"This is it, Carl. All of it. By God, you did it. You actually found it for me. I could kiss you all over." She was bouncing up and down with excitement. Well, part of her was, anyhow.

I turned to the kid. "Can you tell us who rented this space?"

"Sure. We'll need to go to the office to check the files."

"Annabelle, you'd better put that stuff back, and cover it up."

"What? Oh, yeah . . . sure." She seemed distracted.

"What's the matter, Belle? Something bothering you?"

"I just wondered . . . Don't you smell it? What the hell is that?" She wrinkled her nose, looking around.

I took a deep breath and found no enjoyment in it. "Good question. What's the hospital using that smells that bad? Besides the food, I mean." She threw me a dirty look. "Come on, Belle. Cover it up and let's get out of here."

"What? What the hell . . . Oh, yeah. I guess . . ." Some of the excitement went out of her. "We didn't have any authority to come in here, did we? No warrant, or anything like that."

"No, we didn't. If we don't get out of here right now, and let the cops handle this, you may not be able to get the stuff back at all. We have to report this to the authorities, and let them do the actual recovery."

"Yeah. I guess," she agreed, reluctantly.

We followed the kid to the office where he looked through a log book. "Space number 218 was rented out to the Colombian Relief Committee, last July. Some guy by the name of Gomez Adams signed the agreement. Gomez

Friends and Other Perishables

Adams. That name sounds familiar."

"It should. He's been in reruns on television for twenty years. He's in partnership with his Uncle Fester." I shook my head at Annabelle. "It'll still take some work to find out who's responsible for this. Now the question is, how do we let the cops know about it, without getting ourselves in trouble for trespass?"

We all thought that over for a minute, then the kid came up with the solution. "Ms. Hicks, maybe I could do it."

"Do what, Jason?"

"Well, let's say that you and I met casually, a few months ago, and you happened to mention to me that some things were missing from the hospital, and let's say that today I happened to notice some of those things were being stored right here in the warehouse. The normal thing for me to do would be to notify you about it. Then you would just naturally go to the police. They could get a warrant and come out here to check things out."

"That's good, Jason," I said, "but the police need a pretty good reason to get a warrant. They might not want to do that on just your word."

"Okay, then what about this?" He showed us a page in the ledger. "This is a list of all the items stored in space 218. That should match the list of things you're missing, right, Ms. Hicks?"

"I'll be damned," Annabelle muttered.

"What if I fax a copy of this list to your office at the hospital? Just because I thought it looked like the same stuff you 'told' me about?" He paused for effect, grinning. "When you showed them this list, and compared it with your list of stolen things, wouldn't that be enough for a warrant?"

"It damn sure would, Jason," I said. "But what about

you? Aren't you likely to get fired for looking through company files?"

"If he does, he comes right back to work at the hospital," Annabelle promised. "With a fat raise, too. Jason, you've been great, and I won't forget it."

The kid blushed like a school girl and shuffled his feet. I thought he was going to say something like "gosh" or "shucks," but he just grinned.

"We'd better get out of here, Belle. Thanks for your help, Jason. You've been great. And feed that dog of yours, before someone gets eaten." We left him glowing in the office and returned to the van. I dropped Annabelle off at her truck. Before she climbed out of the van, I had another thought.

"Say, Annabelle, I think I know what you might want to check on next."

"Yeah? Well any suggestions are welcome. What'd you have in mind?"

"That smell back there. I finally realized what it was and where it probably came from. I think the canvas tarp covering up the stuff had that smell all through it, and you know, to me that smelled just like a garbage dump."

She thought for a moment and agreed, "Damn, I think you're right. It did smell like garbage, but why?"

"If I were you, I'd check on the possibility they were working with someone who drives a garbage truck. The janitors or maintenance crew could manage to get all that stuff through the hospital hallways and back to the loading docks, couldn't they? Then all they need is an accomplice who backs up to the dock with a garbage truck. They dump the stuff in the back and cover it up with a tarp. Who's going to look through garbage for an iron lung?"

We discussed the possibilities for a few minutes, then it

was time to call it a night.

"Well, C.J., you really came through for me," she said, retrieving her 9mm from beneath the seat. "I can think of a lot of ways to show my gratitude, but I don't suppose your wife would appreciate that."

"No, Belle, she probably wouldn't. But it's a nice thought, and I imagine I'll spend a few nights dreaming about you again, just like I used to."

"Thanks, sweet thing," she said, a little sadly. "It's nice to think someone still dreams about me once in a while."

"Don't sell yourself short, Juicy Fruit. So long."

I waited till she was in her truck, with the motor running, before I drove off. Sherry was still asleep when I got home, undressed, and crawled into bed. She couldn't understand why I was still so sleepy when the alarm went off two hours later.

That afternoon I was in my little office going through the mail when the phone rang. It was Annabelle. She was very happy.

"We got them, C.J., thanks to you. The cops got a warrant early this morning, we went out and recovered all the goods, and then they tracked down the bastards and picked them up just about an hour ago."

"Who was it? An employee, like you thought?"

"Damn right. Gomez Adams turned out to be Manuel Gomez, a janitor here. He was working with his brother, who operates a trash hauling service, and two women who are working as nurses' aides right here in the hospital. They actually had an organization called the Colombia Relief Committee. And get this. You were right. They were starting their own hospital. In Colombia. They needed the equipment and supplies to get started, and they didn't have a damn dime between them to buy the stuff."

"Sounds like their intentions were honorable. You may have a tough time getting them convicted for anything."

"Oh hell, we're not even going to try. Most of the stuff they stole was surplus anyway. I think the Board of Directors is going to work out a deal with them. The hospital will help supply them with the stuff they need down there, and the publicity will be good for our image. Politics in the medical profession, you know how it works."

"Are you okay with that, Belle?"

"Sure. I don't care if they get off, as long as everybody knows I did my job and got the stuff back. With your help, of course."

"You can leave me out of it. The credit is all yours. And Jason's, I guess. Is he going to come out of it okay?"

"You bet. He starts back here on Monday. As a shift supervisor. That's the least I could do. Anybody else would have fed us to that damn dog. By the way, I called the Adams kid and told him we would be delivering his wheelchair this afternoon. I'll make sure he knows you had a hand in getting it back."

"He's going to be mighty happy to get it back."

"Carl, there's something else. When we went through the stuff at the warehouse we found a partially burned X-ray envelope. No X-ray, and most of the envelope was missing, but the patient's name was on the piece left. It was James Walter Jay. I thought you might be interested."

"Damn right I'm interested. Did you ask these guys what they were doing with it?"

"Sure. Gomez said he was paid five hundred dollars to make a swap. Some guy gave him another envelope with a different X-ray in it, and told him to swap that envelope for the one in the file. Gomez did the job, gave the original

X-ray to the man, and collected his fee. The guy pulled the X-ray out of the envelope, looked at it, then set everything on fire. We found what was left."

"This guy have a name?"

"Gomez never did get a name, but he described the guy to me. It sounded like Jimmy all right. And Carl, that's not all. It turned into a regular thing. About once a month Jimmy would contact Gomez and they would pull the same stunt all over again, with different patients. Gomez couldn't remember any patients' names, but you can bet they were all phony injuries. He said that most of the envelopes had a doctor's name on them too, and they were all the same name. He couldn't remember the name, but he said he thought it started with Car, or something like that."

"Something like . . . ? Carlyle! But why would his name be on hospital X-rays?"

"When a doctor submits a request to look at a patient's X-ray, that request becomes part of the history, and is recorded on the envelope. So, does all this mean something to you?"

"It sure does, Belle. Say a man has an accident, in a car wreck, or falls off a ladder, and goes to the emergency room. They take an X-ray, can't find anything seriously wrong, so they give the guy an aspirin and send him home. The X-ray goes into a file. A few days or a few weeks later this guy goes to his chiropractor with a sore back, and says, by the way, I fell off a ladder the other day. If the chiropractor happens to be named Carlyle, he just might talk the patient into a claim for a serious injury, but he has to do something about the original X-ray. You can't fake one, so you make a swap. Now there is evidence to take to court. If it ever gets that far, which it usually doesn't."

"You really think that would work?"

"It would in most cases, because insurance companies don't normally fight a case all the way to court, especially if they think there is evidence of an actual injury. Besides, lawyers cost lots of money, and when you add in the cost of bad publicity, and maybe a bad faith lawsuit, they usually think it's cheaper in the long run to pay up."

"If you say so, C.J., you're the pro."

"Do me a favor, Belle? Would you write down what you told me, put that burned fragment into an envelope and send everything to Detective Albert Sweet, at the Broken Arrow Police Department?"

"Can do. But I think you owe me a dinner."

"Sure. Let me talk to Sherry, and we'll set a date to have you over."

"No thanks. That wasn't exactly what I had in mind, and you damn well know it."

"Yeah. Too bad. You'd like her, and she would . . . No, I guess not. Maybe another time, another place."

"Sure. See you around, C.J."

"Thanks, Belle. Take care." I hung up, leaned back in my chair and, for just a moment, enjoyed a few memories of a sunny day after school when she and I drove out to Turkey Creek, and went skinny dipping. Oh, well . . .

Christmas came and went. It always does, I know, but it still makes my life a hell from about the first day of December until the afternoon I carry all the boxes and ripped paper out to the trash cans. I have a terrible time shopping for Christmas. I can never decide what to buy. Anyone. I know a lot of families give each other hints, or even outright requests, but I grew up thinking Christmas presents were supposed to be a surprise, and I've never been able to get over that. So I spend hours, walking miles, through shopping mall after shopping mall, looking for that perfect gift. Sherry, of course, always starts shopping sometime in late September, and she comes up with terrific gifts for everyone. For instance, one of my gifts from her was a set of bathroom scales, which informed me I had gained six unwanted pounds since the day before Halloween. Terrific.

I spent a lot of time looking for Andrew Baker, but I managed to fit it in around my normal load of investigations and surveillances for Underhill and a few other clients who call upon me regularly. After the murder and mayhem I had been through during the previous four months, all of the cases I worked seemed pretty dull. For that I was truly grateful, but it was still difficult to keep my eyes open during long hours spent waiting for an opportunity to video some poor sap performing physical feats "inconsistent with allegations of injury."

One of my subjects was a guy who claimed a head injury following a fall from a second-story apartment balcony. He was suing the apartment owners for neglect in allowing the balcony railing to come into disrepair. Of course, the fact that he weighed in at better than three hundred forty pounds may have had some effect on the wooden railing, but according to his attorney, that was irrelevant. One interesting thing had happened just two days into my investigation. I had stopped by Worker's Compensation Court to use one of their computer terminals to check my current subject for prior claims. As I was leaving I nearly bumped into Harlan Q. Ridgeway. He was just arriving, and we met at the door to the lobby. He was with a client, a young woman wearing a neck brace and holding onto Ridgeway's arm for support. Her agony was obvious in the way she held her head very still and tilted to one side. She was very conscientious, and well rehearsed, but the look of pain in her expression changed quickly to one of puzzlement when

Ridgeway saw me standing right in front of him and jerked to a halt.

I was mad, to say the least. This kidnapper, this low-life who was ready to see me blown away with a 12-gauge shotgun and had helped dig my grave in a persimmon grove, was still roaming around, practicing law, an "officer of the court." I was looking down at him, into his eyes, trying hard not to touch him, when he turned suddenly very pale, ducked his head, and circled around me to enter the waiting room. Much to my surprise I showed great restraint, and just stood there as he walked away. That probably saved me from spending at least a night in jail.

Even with the taste of Christmas cookies lingering, the new year was upon us, along with the first major snowstorm of the season. Sherry and I agreed long ago that New Years' Eve brought out the amateur drinkers, making it an evening best spent indoors, safely out of harm's way. So we generally let the girls stay with their grandparents while we spend the evening with a small group of close friends, playing board games, nibbling from a buffet of assorted cheeses and appropriate crackers, smoked ham, pepper beef, and bowls of fruit, washed down with sampling sips of domestic wines—all colors and shades. Then at midnight we welcome the new year with imported champagne and caviar, our one evening of shameful extravagance, which prepares us for another year of dieting and budget stretching.

Our guests left by 2:00 A.M., and by 3:00 we finished putting away the leftover food, stored the dirty dishes in the washer, showered, and crawled into bed. By 3:10 we were both asleep. Not very romantic, I suppose, but it was just as well. We were going to need our rest, because January was going to be one hell of a month.

CHAPTER THIRTEEN

The weatherman finally got serious about winter during the first week of the new year. Daytime highs held below thirty degrees, with wind chills in the teens, and the snow lingered. I picked up a new overcoat at an after-Christmas sale, to replace the one that had been ruined when Jimmy shot me in the shoulder. I also had the van and the station wagon winterized just in time, and fixed some problems with the weather stripping around the doors of our old house. It was all very domestic, and I felt just like any other middle-class businessman taking care of chores and looking after the day-to-day needs of his family. Of course, what my family needed most of all was to feel safe again—to be reassured that the big bad man wasn't going to sneak into our home some night and murder us all. So far I hadn't been much help in that area.

It was inevitable that the girls, Pam and Julie, would learn all about the shootings and my involvement. After all, they were both old enough to read, and the local newspaper wasn't shy about printing crime news. That's their job. And the girls knew I had been shot in Oklahoma City, with the Yates woman, but they probably didn't know exactly why. Of course, Sherry and I had always been as honest as we could be in answering questions the girls might ask, no matter how embarrassing or delicate the answers might be, but I wasn't really prepared when the girls confronted us one morning after breakfast, while I was sipping coffee and Sherry was sitting nearby in her favorite chair, reading the morning paper. Jackson was lying in the corner near the fireplace, eating one of my shoes. They came into the living room and stood in front of us, together, almost as though joined at the shoulder. Pam, apparently the delegated spokesperson, asked if they could talk to us "about something," and I said, "Sure, what can we do for you?"

Pam first glanced at her sister for support, then blurted out, "Daddy, why is that man trying to kill you?" As she said it, a single tear escaped the corner of her eye and was quickly rubbed away with a clenched fist.

Sherry quickly put down the paper and moved to the couch. On the way she gathered up both girls in her arms and arranged them on either side of her, hugging them close, and making those comforting sounds only mothers can make.

For the next hour I tried to explain to them how, while doing my job, I had discovered that several people had been involved in a crime, and that they were afraid they might go to jail because of me, and that, even though they had been very mad at me and had tried to "hurt" me before, now that the police knew all about them and what they had done, chances are they wouldn't try to "hurt" me again.

"Daddy, does Mr. Sweet know what they did?" Julie asked, her eyes big and round in expectation.

"Yes he does, and he's going to do everything he can to see that they are punished."

"Boy," Julie shook her head, "I'll bet they're scared of him."

"Yes, I'm sure they are." Sherry caught my eye with a slight shake of her head, and reading her correctly I quickly added, "Of course, the only reason they have to be afraid of him, or any police officer, is because they have committed crimes, and they don't want to be punished."

"Daddy?"

"Yes, Pam?"

She was looking at the floor when she said, "The kids at school said you shot someone. Did you?"

It was getting tougher and tougher, but I couldn't lie to them. "Yes, sweetheart, I did. I didn't want to, but I had to."

"The man was shooting at your father, honey. Daddy had to defend himself," Sherry said softly.

"Was it Uncle Jimmy?" Pam asked, not really wanting to know.

"Uhf. Yes, sweetheart. I think someone forced Uncle Jimmy to try to shoot me. I'm sure he didn't really want to do it, but he thought he had to. It was late at night, and very dark. I couldn't see who was shooting at me. I shot back, and later I found out it was . . . Uncle Jimmy."

There were quite a few more tears after that, from all of us, but we eventually talked it out, and I suppose the girls were somewhat reassured. I think even Sherry felt a lot better after our family discussion and the concluding "pep talk." I was wishing I did.

That had been on a Saturday morning, before the girls went back to school on the following Monday. Things were almost back to normal. I was working, Sherry was working, the girls were working too, in their own way. Then, three weeks into January, our world began to shake.

It was Friday night. I had been working surveillance all day on a twenty-eight-year-old playboy who had filed a back injury claim after an automobile accident. He alleged he couldn't walk without crutches, and so far I hadn't been able to prove he was lying. Granted, he did take a date to a local nightclub, but while I was inside the club watching him, he stayed seated in a booth, cuddled up with an attractive blonde, his crutches sharing the booth. He never approached the dance floor, which was just as well, since I couldn't carry the video camera around inside the club anyway. People in those places are often touchy about having their pictures taken.

I left the club and the young couple a little after 2:00 A.M., and headed home. The house was dark when I pulled into the drive, and I was careful not to make too much noise as I tripped over Jackson, the dog, on my way to the kitchen. I wanted to drink a glass of milk and put away a cheese sandwich before going upstairs to bed. Jackson was hungry too. So hungry he overcame his usual nervousness around me and allowed me to feed him a slice of cheese, a couple of slices of bologna, a wedge of apple, and half a dozen grapes.

I was just getting ready to turn out the kitchen light when the front doorbell rang. My watch told me it was 3:00 in the morning, and I had to assume the person at the door didn't have a watch. If he did, he would be home in bed.

The .45 automatic was in my hand as I peeked through a front window to see who our visitor was. I still had it in my hand when I opened the door and let Joy Carlyle into the living room. After making sure there was no one else on the porch, I locked the front door and turned to ask her what the hell she thought she was doing.

"I'm sorry," she stammered. "I just didn't know where else to go. They're going to kill me."

"Who is? And why should I care?"

"Please, sugar, I know what you must think of me, but I never wanted them to hurt you, honest. I couldn't do anything, could I? Those bastards don't listen to me." While she was talking she paced around the room, like a wild animal in a cage. She was scared, and I was thinking perhaps I was on the verge of breaking the fraud case wide open. "Can I have a cigarette, please?"

"I'm sorry, Joy, I don't smoke."

"Terrific. That's just great. I run out of the house half-dressed, no purse, no money, and no cigarettes, and wouldn't you know the guy I run to doesn't smoke."

"Half . . . what? Half dressed did you say . . . ?" I finally noticed she was wearing a black, knee-length cloth coat, with the collar turned up against the cold. It was a nice coat, probably expensive, but it was a little incongruous with the pink house shoes she had on. "Joy, how did you get here?"

"I flagged a cab. The driver was a sweet little old man who stopped at a convenience store long enough for me to look up your address in the phone book, then he brought me here."

"But you said you didn't have any money. Why would he . . ."

"Like I said, sugar, he was a sweet little old man. I asked him real nice, and promised I would look him up later to settle the tab. Then I showed him that I didn't have anything with me, and he agreed to trust me." She giggled, nervously. "Men usually do trust me if I ask them to. You trust me, don't you, sugar?" As she said it, she opened the coat and let it slip off her shoulders and fall to the floor. She had been telling the truth when she said she was only half dressed, and I could see why the cabby agreed to trust her. The blue push-up lace bra was a little redundant, since she obviously didn't need any help in that area, and the lace panties were a perfect complement to . . . everything. But in spite of the over-all effect, which was staggering, I certainly would not have trusted her, under any circumstances. But of course I knew her better than the cabby had.

I bent to retrieve the coat. "Come on, Joy, cover it up. I'm immune. You're wasting your time."

She turned away, moving across the room to sit in my favorite chair, with her legs curled beneath her. "Don't be mean, sugar. I can help you, you know, if you will help me."

"What do you want, Joy? And keep your voice down." I suddenly remembered I had a wife and two daughters asleep upstairs.

"Too late," Sherry called from the stairway. "Carl, why didn't you tell me we had company?" She sounded fine, and looked fine. She had taken time to comb her hair, and she was wearing a short black silk robe over lounging pajamas that were sheer enough to show off her legs. Yeah, she looked great, all right, but there was a chill in her voice.

Joy had the sense to look embarrassed as I introduced them. "Sherry, this is Joy Carlyle, Doctor Carlyle's wife. I believe I've mentioned her before. Joy, this is my wife, Sherry."

Sherry crossed to Joy with her hand out. "Good evening. Or is it good morning? So nice to meet you. No, please don't get up, dear. You must be freezing. Carl, perhaps you should light the fireplace."

I ignored that, and handed Joy her coat. As she slipped it on she said, "I'm sorry. I had no idea he was married. I mean it never occurred to me. He just doesn't act like a married man."

"I know," Sherry replied. "I haven't had time to get him fully trained yet. But I'm still working on him. Now, what's this about someone trying to kill you?"

Joy turned back to me. "I heard them talking. They thought I was asleep, but I wasn't. Andrew started it, and that damn Harlan was all for it, but Stanley said no, and

Friends and Other Perishables

stood up for me at first. Then when Andrew threatened to put Stanley in the ground with me, he backed down . . . the louse."

"You're talking about Andrew Baker? He's with your husband and Ridgeway now?" I guess I said it a little too loud, and she suddenly looked scared again.

"Yeah. They were a little while ago."

"Where? At your place?"

"Yeah, sure. I don't dress—or undress—like this anywhere else. At least, not any more I don't," she said, glancing at Sherry.

"Why would your husband and the others want to kill you?" Sherry asked.

"Andrew heard me talking to Stanley. I was telling him we should try to make a deal with the cops. If we turned in Harlan and Andrew, and told them where the money is, maybe they would let us go. We could even maybe get a reward, or something." She looked like she was going to cry. "Damn it, I don't want to go to jail. I'm too pretty."

Sherry turned to me. "Carl, why don't you call the police and let them know where to pick up Andy?" She looked like she was afraid I'd go after them myself. She knew me pretty well.

"You do that. I can't just sit around here, I'm going to go make sure they don't get away before the cops get there. And call Sweet. He deserves to know about this. Joy will give you the address. Will you and the girls be all right?"

"The girls aren't here. They're spending the weekend with their grandparents. It's Mom's birthday. Carl, please be careful. Wait for the police to get there."

"I will, if I can." I indicated Joy with a glance. "Watch after things while I'm gone. And you be careful, too."

"I can handle it," she said, and I believed her.

I left hurriedly through the kitchen, grabbing my new overcoat from the rack near the door. The van was still warm, so I slid behind the wheel and headed for the Carlyle house. They lived in a large two-story brick home near 21st and Peoria, a plush, high-dollar neighborhood. Carlyle's neighbors were going to be shocked when they read about him in the paper.

I cut the headlights as I turned into Carlyle's driveway and headed for the house, at least 150 feet back from the road. The house was dark, except for light showing through a set of French doors at the southwest corner of the ground floor. I was surprised to see there were no cars in the drive in front of the house. I started wondering if I was too late.

I let the Chevy coast to a stop, slid out from behind the wheel, and closed the door quietly behind me. The gravel drive made loud crunching noises beneath my feet as I moved toward the lights. After scrambling over a low rock wall, I found myself on a small patio just outside the French doors. The curtains were partially drawn, but there was enough of a gap to let me see inside. The room was obviously an office, with a desk, bookshelves, and two leather wingback chairs. There were no sounds and no movement inside. I reached for the door handle, with no expectation of it being unlocked, and was surprised to feel it slide open. I stepped inside, the automatic ready in my right hand. I almost shot my own reflection, visible in a large mirror hanging on the opposite wall, and just as my nerves were starting to settle down, I saw his feet sticking out from behind the desk. I wasn't too alarmed, because his toes were pointed toward the ceiling.

It was Carlyle. Or it had been Carlyle. He was dead, his shirt front stained with blood. He had taken at least one, possibly several rounds in the chest. He was still warm. I

Friends and Other Perishables

was the one getting cold.

I worked my way through the house quickly, but there was no one there. The first squad car arrived moments later, and after the usual process of my being held at gunpoint, disarmed, questioned, and identified, they went about their business of securing the crime scene and calling in for more help.

It was almost an hour before Sweet arrived, and his mood was as bad as mine. "Another corpse. Thanks, Jacobs, just what we needed."

"I didn't shoot him. I started to, just for the hell of it, but I didn't want to confuse the coroner with an extra slug in the body. Go pick on someone your own size."

Sweet, like me, was more of an observer than a participant. He was out of his jurisdiction, and while the local police all knew him, and respected him, he stayed out of their way while they searched the house, dusted for prints, and eventually bagged Carlyle's body for transport. He discussed events with the investigating officers, among them Detective Sergeant Samuel Fry. They stood just out of my hearing, glancing my way occasionally, with some glances less friendly than others. Finally, Fry walked over to me. "Jacobs, you say Carlyle's wife is at your place?"

"Yeah. My wife is looking after her. She was pretty shook up. Like I told you, she was sure Baker and Ridgeway, and her husband as well, were all planning to kill her, to stop her from talking to the cops. She was looking for a reward—and immunity, of course."

"What makes you think she didn't pop her husband? She could have made up the whole thing about Baker and Ridgeway," he said, skeptically.

"What makes you think she isn't telling the truth?"

"Well, for one thing, I sent a car to your place to pick

her up, and she's not there. Apparently, she took off."

"Apparently? Didn't Sherry know where she was?"

"I don't know, Jacobs. Your wife wasn't there, either. The place was empty. At least, no one came to the door."

I almost laughed at him, thinking he must be mistaken, or have the wrong address, or something. After all, just a short time before, I had left Sherry and Joy together, at the house. Sherry had called the police, and even got hold of Sweet. They wouldn't go anywhere, not in the middle of the night. Not unless . . . And suddenly I was very cold.

I ran out of the house to my car. I heard Sweet yelling at me, but I ignored him. I threw gravel all over several police cars parked in the drive and even had to pull out onto the lawn to get past the coroner's station wagon. I would have driven over it if necessary. One thought kept running through my mind. She wouldn't have left the house if she didn't have to. She wouldn't have left the house in the middle of the night. If she didn't answer the door when the cops were there, either she wasn't there, or else she was . . . No, I wasn't prepared to go there. She just wasn't at home, that's all. And if she wasn't home, then she was somewhere else, somewhere she didn't want to be, and somewhere I didn't want her to be.

She must be with Joy. Baker and Ridgeway wanted Joy dead, so if they had any idea she had gone to my place, then they would look for her there. And since they weren't at the Carlyle house, and since they had murdered Carlyle before they left, then there was nothing to keep them from going to my house and killing Joy there. And if they killed Joy there, they might as well . . .

It was still before dawn, and there was little traffic on the streets, not that it would have made any difference. Sweet and I arrived back at the house in record time, in separate cars. He had the advantage of a siren. I just didn't give a damn. I ran through the house checking every room, but Sherry wasn't there. Neither was Joy. The front room looked undisturbed, at first. I found two coffee cups, half empty, on the coffee table in front of the couch. The coffee was cold. A thermos in the kitchen held about half a pot of still warm coffee, and there was a package of sweet rolls sitting open on the counter. Two rolls were missing. Apparently Sherry and Joy had breakfast before they disappeared. Well, at least they weren't hungry.

Back in the living room Sweet was on the phone, talking to someone at the police station. "They're gone. Nothing seems to be disturbed, but her car is in the driveway, and all the lights were on. Just a minute . . ." He caught my attention and pointed at the front door. We had come in through the kitchen, and I hadn't noticed before. The door frame was splintered around the lock.

"It looks like someone kicked in the front door," Sweet continued into the phone. "Put out an all points on Baker and Ridgeway, as well as Carlyle's wife . . . and Mrs. Jacobs. She's about thirty, five-two, one hundred twenty-five pounds, brown and brown. She was wearing . . ."

I shook my head. "Last time I saw her she was wearing a black silk robe over black pajamas. She might have changed, though."

"Just put clothing description unknown. Keep me posted, will you, Ray? Thanks." He hung up and looked around the room. "What about Pam and Julie?"

"They're with their grandparents. Spending the weekend, thank God."

"Except for the door, nothing's been disturbed. No struggle, or anything," he said, encouragingly.

"No, no struggle. That's supposed to be good, right? So,

either they left willingly, or at least quietly, or else they were carried out by those two bastards."

"Come on, Carl. If they were going to hurt the women they wouldn't have bothered to take them anywhere. We would have found them right here."

"So, why the hell would they take them?" I demanded. "And where? I can see why they might want Joy dead. I mean, she can testify against them in court. She knows everything. But what the hell do they want with Sherry? All she knows is what I've told her, and God knows that hasn't been much, because I don't know very much myself."

"Maybe they want her as leverage against you. Or they may think they'll need hostages if we find them. Hell, I don't know. Maybe they just like pretty women."

"So, let's go find them." I was moving toward the door.

Sweet stopped me in my tracks with a question. "Go where? Where do you suggest we look first?"

I was saved from having to come up with an answer by sounds outside, signifying the arrival of several squad cars. Detective Fry pushed open the front door and walked in, pausing long enough to examine the broken door frame. He was followed by three uniforms and a couple guys in rumpled suits who started taking pictures and sprinkling fingerprint powder over everything.

"I'm sorry to hear about your wife, Jacobs, but we'll find her. Any idea where she might be?"

I turned and walked away without answering. In the kitchen I poured myself a cup of lukewarm coffee from the thermos and stood over the sink drinking it. Sweet came in behind me, picked up a sweet roll, and leaned against the counter, putting away the roll in three bites.

"She'll be okay, Jacobs. You have to keep telling yourself that. Thinking anything else will just drive you crazy."

"I'm crazy now, because I'm so damn helpless. And so are you, and all those clowns in there messing up my house. What good are they going to do? We know what happened, we know who has her. We just don't know where she is, Goddamnit!" I slammed my hand against the counter top in frustration. Sweet licked his fingers, took a glass from the cabinet, and helped himself to the milk in the fridge.

"Did that help? Feel better now?"

I ignored him and went over to sit at the kitchen table. He pulled out the chair across from me, where Sherry usually sat. The chair groaned as he lowered his bulk onto it. "All we can do is wait, Carl. We're both pretty good at that, aren't we? We've done enough of it in our time. Wait and watch. Plan and daydream. What if this, or what if that? If this happens I'll do it one way, if something else happens, I'll . . . well, you know, right?"

Yeah, I knew. But I never had to sit and wait and worry and wonder if my wife was still alive.

Fry walked in and brought us up to date. "Well, the neighbors didn't hear or see anything. That's not surprising, considering it's just now getting light outside. You'll be happy to know that the lab boys can't find anything that looks like blood, so chances are both women are okay. At least, they weren't hurt when they left. There's a footprint on the face of the door where someone kicked it open. We'll be able to match the print easily, whenever we catch them. Assuming he's still wearing the same shoe, of course."

"And then, of course, you'll be able to charge him with breaking and entering. Assuming I haven't gotten to him first," I shouted angrily, getting into Fry's face. Sweet pulled me back and sat me down in the chair as easily as I might have handled one of my daughters.

"He's a little upset, Fry. What with his wife missing and all. I'm sure you understand."

"Yeah, sure. No harm done. Look, Mr. Jacobs, I'm sorry if I don't sound concerned. I am, really, it's just that this job . . . you know how it is. I can't let myself get all worked up every time some nice person gets into trouble. I'd go nuts. I've got a job to do, and I do it the best way I know how. And I'm pretty good at it, too. Just have a little patience with us, okay?"

I was still choking on anger, but I realized I was directing it in the wrong direction. "Yeah. Yes, Detective Fry, I know. I'm sorry. Like Sweet says, I'm just upset."

"Well, no blood, no foul, right? We're about finished here, Mr. Jacobs, and we'll get out of your hair. Let us know if your wife turns up. They may simply let her go, you know? She's liable to call home any minute and ask you to come and pick her up. If that happens, give us a call. And, we'll keep you advised from our end. You coming, Sweet?"

"No. I'll be heading home in a minute. I'd appreciate it if you would keep our office informed, Fry." Sweet has a way of asking for favors that people find hard to ignore.

"Sure, Sweet, no problem. Professional courtesy, and all that. Good night. Good night, Mr. Jacobs." He turned and left toward the living room, gathering up his crew on the way.

Sweet left a short time later, after having assured me everything possible was going to be done to find Sherry. And Joy, of course. He advised me to stay put, near the phone, so that he, or Fry, or Sherry could reach me quickly. It made sense, and I agreed to do so. Hard to do, but where else could I go?

The house was empty and quiet by 7:00 A.M., and I sat in the living room, in front of the fireplace, with the phone on my lap, eventually falling asleep like that. Shortly after 9:30 A.M. the phone rang, waking me up from a fitful sleep. I was startled and confused when I answered the phone. As soon as I recognized the voice, I was just angry.

"Jacobs, I'm sure you know who this is. Are the police gone?"

"Yes, you son-of-a-bitch, they're gone. Where's my wife?"

"She's here, with me. She's fine, Jacobs. I've got nothing against her. In fact, I've always found her quite attractive, in a domineering sort of way. I prefer my women a little more humble, though."

"Listen to me, Baker. If you hurt her, I will hunt you down and kill you in cold blood. Do you understand? I'm not saying I will hurt you, or even beat you to a pulp. I will kill you. No arrest, no police. There will be no trial. No attorney to get you off. Nothing like that. You will simply die a slow and painful death. Do you understand?"

"Sure, Carl, I understand. I can call you Carl, can't I? We've known each other long enough for that. In fact, I've know you for so long that I'll wager, given the chance at me, you would not cause me to face a 'slow and painful death' as you put it, but would, in fact, kill me rather quickly. I don't think you have the temperament or the patience for torture and slow death. Am I right?"

I couldn't force words around the emotions choking me.

He didn't wait for my answer but went on prodding me with that soft, greasy voice of his. "No, I don't think you would. On the other hand, I am different. I have that cold streak in me that would allow me to do such a thing. Torture, I mean. Even to someone I might care for, under other circumstances. Someone like Sherry, for instance. She is very lovely, and usually enjoyable to be around at work. She dresses well, and I like those short skirts she wears. Very flattering. And the outfit she is wearing now is very . . . effective, I suppose I should say. Very sheer and sexy. I always have liked black lingerie. But that won't protect her from me, if you don't do as I say." His manner, while casual, had turned decidedly cold and menacing.

"What do you want, Baker?"

"Well, it's like this. You see, my friends and I have put away quite a lot of cash for just such a turn of events as we have experienced recently. Thanks to your meddling. But we can't get to it right now. We would be seen and arrested, and that is not in my plans. So, I want you to get the money and bring it to us. It's very simple, really."

"Where is all this money that you can't get to without being seen?"

"Why, where else would it be, dear boy, but at our club. Our country club, in my locker. Stanley and Harlan and I are all members of the Westridge Country Club. Of course, they probably will deny they ever heard of us when word of this gets out, but I don't mind, really. They're not my type, never were. I was going to resign, anyway."

"I'm sure they'll be glad to hear that. Of course, Stanley has already dropped out, hasn't he? Do you suppose they'll miss him?"

"Not at all. Even though Stanley seemed to fit in there better than I, or even better than Harlan, he never was a very likable person."

"Is that why you killed him?"

"Actually, that was Harlan. Not that it matters. I was there, after all, and according to the law, I am just as responsible. Poor Stanley. He did so love money, it's a shame he didn't live to spend it all. I guess his wife will have to spend it for him, if she manages to live through this."

Friends and Other Perishables

"Is she there? Is she all right?"

"It's thoughtful of you to ask, dear boy, and I'll tell her you did so. Yes, she is fine, also. Well, not fine, I suppose. Harlan got into the scotch a short time ago, and he simply can't hold his liquor. He lost his temper when Joy called him a few choice names, and he . . . well, he struck her, several times, and . . . shall we say . . . had his way with her. I was out of the room, tending to other matters, so I wasn't here to stop him. I assure you I spoke to him rather harshly about his behavior, and he regrets his actions. It was a shame though, that your wife had to watch. It must have been very distressing for her, to lie there, helpless, while he . . . well, never mind."

"Baker, you bastard, you keep him away from her. If any harm comes to her, I will hold you responsible."

"Of course you will. I understand. Now, are you ready for your instructions?"

"Go ahead."

"Go to the Westridge clubhouse and into the men's locker room. Just pretend you belong there. Security is pretty lax. Go to locker number 215. There is a combination lock on the door. You better write this down. Right three times to fifteen, left twice to twenty-two, then back right to three. Got that?"

"I've got it, damn you."

"There is a blue nylon bag in the locker. It is stuffed full of hundred-dollar bills. Really quite lovely, all that money. It's just an emergency fund, of course—we have the bulk of our funds in banks, outside the country. But we need the cash to, as they say, make our getaway. Bring it to me, here. When you arrive, you will be tied up and we will leave you and your lovely wife, and the bruised but still delightful Joy, bound and gagged. Someone will find you soon. After all,

187

the police know about our little hideout. They simply haven't thought to look there yet."

"What hideout? Where are you?"

"I'm so sorry. Didn't I say? We're at the cabin, out at Keystone Lake. Or we will be, soon after I hang up. You've been there once before, I understand. Think you can find it again?"

"How could I find the damn cabin again? I was unconscious most of the time and rolled up on the floor with a blanket over my head. No, I couldn't find the damn cabin."

"Please, Carl, relax. It's really very easy." He gave me brief directions, west on highway 51 past Sand Springs, crossing the Keystone dam and on toward Mannford until I reached a gravel road leading north.

When I finally had a good idea where they were, I interrupted him. "Okay, I'll be there as soon as I can. Just don't let anything happen to my wife. Or Joy, either."

"Nothing will happen to anyone if you do as you're told. You have one hour. No, I'll be generous, make it an hour and a half. Just remember, that hole my friends dug for you is still out there. It's big enough for two small, shapely bodies, and I can fill it quickly and easily if you fail to carry out your instructions. And Carl, surely I don't think I have to tell you to come alone. We will be watching for uninvited company. If you bring the police, the women will pay for your mistake. I think that's plain enough, don't you?"

Yes, I would say that it was.

CHAPTER FOURTEEN

Even though I was in a hurry, before I left the house I grabbed an extra seven-round magazine for the .45 automatic and took time to tape the little .38 caliber Smith & Wesson revolver to my left ankle. I had underestimated Baker for years, considering him an irritating little jerk my wife had to put up with on the job. But now I knew better. Given any chance at all, I was going to take him out. And, considering the mood I was in, Ridgeway wasn't very likely to survive the day, either. Obviously there was much more to Baker than I had thought. He was too damn smart, and dangerous, to take for granted, and if he gave me even half a chance . . .

Yeah, "if." I knew damn well they weren't going to give me any chance at all. Baker could spout all he wanted to about leaving us tied up while they made their getaway, but I wasn't stupid enough to believe him. As Sherry had said, there were bodies all over the damn place, and a couple more wouldn't matter. Besides, he was out of business and on the run. He wouldn't feel well disposed toward the person responsible for that.

I took the station wagon instead of the van. I was going to the county club to pick up a bag of money, and I thought the van would be inappropriate in that setting. It was just as well I did. At the entrance to the grounds, I had to talk my way past the gate guard, a heavy-set elderly man in a gray, too-small uniform. He was stern, but accepted my story about meeting my employer, "Mr. Williams," for a business luncheon. I picked the name out of the air, knowing there would be at least one Williams on the membership list.

The men's locker room was almost empty. There was still snow on the ground, and it was too cold for even the most avid golfers, so the few members who were at the club were probably playing bridge or sipping bloody marys somewhere. I fumbled with the combination lock, making three attempts before the damn thing opened. Sure enough, in the bottom of the locker I found a blue nylon sports bag, and it was heavy. I didn't examine the contents until I was back in the station wagon. There were several bundles of hundreds, and many more bundles of twenties. I estimated at least fifty thousand bucks.

I waved to the guard on the way out, but he wasn't interested in me anymore. Traffic wasn't too bad, and before long I was on highway 51, westbound. There are long stretches of four-lane divided highway from Tulsa to the Keystone Lake resort area. A trip that normally takes thirty minutes can be made in fifteen if you don't get stopped by the highway patrol, or by the back-end of a semi. I was out to set a record, but it was one of the longest drives of my life. My wife, the woman I loved, was in the hands of two madmen. Men who had already killed several times, and who, no doubt, would kill again given the least excuse. I had every reason to believe either of them would welcome the chance to kill me. And denied that opportunity, they would readily settle for Sherry's death, knowing what she meant to me.

In times like that I think the body and reflexes take over for us, making up for the fact that our minds are somewhere else. I don't remember seeing anything at all on that drive. I don't remember getting on the expressway, or the traffic, or the patches of ice, or what exit I took. I wasn't thinking at all. I was only remembering.

I remembered the first time Sherry agreed to go out with me, though it certainly wasn't the first time I had asked her. She had turned me down for lunch, for drinks, for a picnic, for dinner and a movie, and had simply laughed when I asked her if she liked baseball. I still don't know if I just wore down her resistance, or if she really was interested in farm sales. That's right, I invited her to go with me to a farm sale, an auction held on a three-hundred-acre farm south of Tulsa, near Okmulgee.

I had been going to farm sales and auctions since I was eighteen and started collecting spurs. By accident I had come across a pair of very old silver Spanish spurs in an antique store in Tulsa. I had been fascinated by the tale the store owner told about how the spurs had belonged to an infamous Mexican bandit who raided back and forth across the Rio Grande for years and had never been caught by authorities on either side of the border. He had reportedly died in a hotel room in Ft. Smith, Arkansas, in 1902, at the age of ninety-five. On his deathbed he gave the spurs to a young boy who swept the floor and emptied spittoons at the hotel, and the boy had passed them on to his son, and so on. Somehow they ended up in the little antique store, where I used to go to look at them twice a week for over a month until I had saved up enough money to buy them and rushed to the store, only to find they had been sold the day before. After that, when I saw something I liked, I either bought it on the spot, or I turned my back and forgot about it. Never again did I spend weeks longing for something I might not be able to have. Until I met Sherry.

At work one day I mentioned casually that I was going to spend Saturday morning at a farm sale. Sherry overheard me and asked what a farm sale was. I explained to her that every once in a while an area farmer or rancher would decide he was tired of fighting floods and drought, bugs and disease, and bottomed out markets and would sell out everything he owned at an auction to raise enough money for his family to start over somewhere else. She seemed so interested, I finally asked her if she would like to go with me. With only a moment's hesitation, she said yes.

For the rest of the week I was certain she was going to back out, but on Saturday morning I drove by her apartment, and she was ready to go. She came to the door wearing a pale green dress and high heels. I was wearing a sweatshirt and jeans. We looked at each other for a second, then started laughing at the same time. From that time on, there was never an awkward moment between us. She changed into a red western shirt and jeans, and before we left the apartment, she put together a picnic lunch.

The day had been a wonderful success. At the auction I bought two pair of spurs, and Sherry picked up a vase she said was perfect for her bedroom. Then I bought a stuffed teddy bear and gave it to her, and she bought a tiny boat in a glass bottle for me.

During a break in the auction we walked a few hundred yards off and spread a blanket under a huge cottonwood tree by a farm pond and had our picnic. From where we were you could see almost all three hundred acres of the farm, the house and barn, the corrals, and a tree house the owner had built for his children. Sherry looked around, and suddenly her eyes filled with tears. She cried quietly as we both empathized with the family, feeling the pain they must have felt being forced to leave that place and all their things. After that neither of us wanted to go back to the auction and buy up any more of the family's belongings. We didn't talk much during the drive back to town. On the way, we both realized we were in love.

I followed the directions Baker had provided and eventually arrived at the cabin. In the daylight it was even bigger and nicer than I had thought. And the view from the porch, looking out over a cliff toward the lake, must have been wonderful, but I didn't notice. What I did notice was Baker, standing in the front doorway, behind the screen. I slid out of the station wagon, the nylon bag in my hand, and stood there watching him. He smiled, then motioned to one side with his undersized chin. I glanced that way and saw Ridgeway pointing a rifle at me from behind a clump of brush. I moved slowly toward the cabin, and up the porch steps. Baker backed away from the door, keeping his eyes on me. He held what looked like a Colt revolver in his right hand, down at his side. As I pulled the screen door open and stepped inside, Baker was pointing the revolver at Sherry's head.

She was sitting on the bare wood floor, her back against a large brightly colored couch, positioned in front of a fireplace. The flickering light from the fire was reflected in tear streaks on her cheeks. Her hands were in front of her, taped at the wrists with what looked like duct tape. There was a similar strip of tape across her mouth and one around her ankles. She was still wearing the short black robe over the sheer pajama bottoms, but the robe was unbuttoned, and I could see red marks on her throat and the side of one breast. I turned toward Baker, taking one step forward, and he pulled back the hammer on the Colt, still pointed at Sherry. "She's not hurt, Jacobs. She was just roughed up a little. When she heard you were coming she started worrying about what might happen to you. She went wild and started kicking and cussing Harlan. He got a little rough, but she's okay, so just calm down before you force me to do something I don't want to do."

I took a deep breath and looked back at Sherry. She shook her head and shrugged her shoulders, as though to say, "What can you do?" I felt the anger start to grow, and a flush washed over me from my forehead to my toes. Suddenly I was relaxed and calm.

"I'm here, Baker. What now?" I heard only a slight noise behind me before I felt a crashing blow against the back of my skull, and the floor slapped me in the face.

When I woke up I was lying across the room from Sherry, my back against the bottom step of a stairway leading upward to the second floor. Baker was still standing over her. I couldn't have been out more than a few minutes. I could see Ridgeway in the center of the room, holding the rifle he had hit me with. I had been hit in the head so many times in the last few months I figured my brain was turning into porridge, but the way things had been going so far, that might be an improvement. In the brief time I was out, someone had tied my hands behind my back and tied my ankles together. A rope ran from my ankles to the stairway banister, effectively tethering me in position.

Ridgeway looked different, somehow, and he certainly acted differently. This Ridgeway wasn't the same self-conscious lawyer who had balked at shooting me the last time I had been here. His face was flushed and alive. He was very animated, his eyes blinking rapidly, shifting his weight from one foot to the other, back and forth, sometimes rocking on his heels. He giggled.

"That does it, right? That son-of-a-bitch won't cause us any more trouble now. I should have blown him away when I had the chance. We wouldn't be in this mess." He moved across the floor toward me. "But it's never too late. I've got a second chance to do you, you bastard."

I barely had time to expel my breath and tense my stomach muscles before the toe of his scuffed dress shoe drove into my gut. He drew back his foot and kicked again, catching the side of my face. I started to black out, but the pain kept me conscious.

"Harlan, that's enough. Damnit, I said enough. You'll have your fun later. Bring that bag over here."

Ridgeway picked up the nylon bag from the floor and walked across the room to join Baker at a table near the front windows. They started pulling the bundles of cash out of the bag and laying them out on the table. I turned toward Sherry and saw she was looking at me. The tears had started again, and I smiled at her to show her I was all right. It probably wasn't a very pretty smile, as I could taste the blood running down my face into the corner of my mouth. After a moment I noticed Joy, too. She was curled up in a chair at the end of the couch. Her face looked even worse than I was sure mine did. Both her eyes were black, and she had been bleeding from the nose and mouth. She was either dead or unconscious, I couldn't tell which. Someone had tossed a blanket over her, but her bare feet stuck out from under the blanket and I could see her ankles were tied, and on the floor next to the chair I saw a small pile of crumpled blue material which looked like the bra and panties she had been wearing earlier. Ridgeway had really worked her over. I was beginning to think I would take him out before I got to Baker. Either one was going to be a pleasure. Baker's voice interrupted my train of thought with words I had hoped I wouldn't hear.

"Did you search him for weapons?"

Ridgeway's startled expression was enough answer, and Baker quickly crossed to me. He found the .45 in the belt holster almost immediately, and turned to give Ridgeway a look that might have shriveled a more sensitive man. He then proceeded to pat me down, emptying my pockets of everything, including the extra magazine for the .45, my wallet, loose change, keys, everything. He eventually found the .38 taped to my ankle. He ripped it off, grinning down at me. "You clever bastard. You figured if I found the automatic, I would stop looking. I'm not as stupid as you might think." He dumped everything except the .45 into a pile on a small table near the door.

Ridgeway called out, "Look for a knife, too. The son-of-a-bitch used a knife on Stanley."

Baker went through all my pockets again. "No knife on him now."

"That's right, I remember, it broke off in Stanley's shoulder." He giggled again. "You should have heard him scream." Watching him closely, I decided Ridgeway had snapped. The pressure and the fear had sent him over the edge. I thought he might even be more dangerous than Baker.

As though reading my mind, Baker confirmed my thought. "As you can see, Harlan has undergone an attitude adjustment. He used to be rather frightened and insecure. A strange condition for a successful attorney, don't you think? But now, of course, his true nature has come forth. He is strong and completely ruthless."

"And completely crazy," I said, watching Ridgeway closely.

"Oh, I think that may be a little harsh. Harlan has been a bit upset lately, naturally, what with having to shoot a close friend like Stanley and all."

"And why did he have to shoot Carlyle?" I already had a good idea why.

"We had all decided Joy was a liability. She thought she

could turn us in for a reward and immunity from prosecution. She may have, at that, but we overheard her discussing it with Stanley. He was against the idea, and I honor his memory for that, but when it was decided Joy had to be eliminated, he balked. It would seem she has a considerable talent, as well as stamina, when it comes to pleasing a man, and she pleased Stanley greatly. He simply wasn't prepared to give her up. So, it was inevitable that he had to go, too. I think Harlan was as surprised as Stanley when the gun he was pointing at Stanley went off. But afterwards, when Harlan realized what comfort there is in a small handgun, and what a feeling of power one derives from killing a man . . . well, he was more or less converted, you see? He likes it. The killing, I mean. He is anxious to kill you, you know. He was somewhat upset at first, after killing Stanley, but that would upset anyone, don't you think—killing a friend? But of course, you should know that as well as anyone, shouldn't you? You had to shoot a good friend, just like Harlan did. That must have been difficult for you."

"You prick."

"Sticks and stones, dear boy. Yes, I suppose that was my fault. I sent Jimmy after you. You may take comfort in the knowledge that he didn't want to do it. In fact, he absolutely refused to kill you, until I pointed out that he had killed that other detective, Foster, and that I would make sure he took the fall for that murder, if any of us were ever arrested. But it was only just. It was Jimmy's fault that Foster ever started looking into the matter in the first place. Jimmy had not followed instructions after we had filed his injury claim. He had started running around without his brace much too soon, and he even bragged about it to a few of his friends. The damn fool still thought of it as a lark. He didn't realize how very important it was to us, Ridgeway and Carlyle and me, that we not attract attention to our business activities."

"Just out of curiosity, Baker, how long has this been going on?"

"How long? On various levels, about eight years, I would say, and several millions of dollars for each of us. It's been very rewarding. Until now." He paused, looking at me thoughtfully. Everything got very quiet as I stared into his moist eyes. I could hear the fire crackle and Sherry breathing rapidly around the gag as Baker raised my own .45 automatic, pressed the muzzle against my forehead, and snapped off the safety. Sherry stopped breathing, I stopped breathing, and I think, so did Baker. The whole damn world held its collective breath as we waited for the automatic to go off. We waited for a very long time, and then Ridgeway giggled. Baker twitched at the obscene sound of it, and I thought he was pulling the trigger, but instead he lowered the pistol, took a deep breath, and smiled at me. "No, not yet."

After I started breathing again I said, "Baker, you told me if I brought you the money you'd leave us here, tied up. You might as well, you know. We can't hurt you anymore. It could be days before anyone found us. Hell, you could be in Spain, or Brazil, or any damn place you want to by then."

"Really, Carl, you didn't believe me, did you? I have been wanting to see you dead for so long now, I simply can't pass up the chance. Jimmy couldn't do it, and even my hired professional couldn't handle the job. The damn fool came highly recommended, too, and cost me a lot of money. But you just stumbled along, protected by some invisible wall of stupidity and ineptitude. You should have figured it out days, even months, earlier. You really should be embarrassed, you know."

"Then, let Sherry go, damnit. She's been your friend, Andy. You worked together, side by side, day after day. She's never harmed you, in any way. Let her go."

He actually seemed to be considering it, for a moment. Then he shook his head.

"No, she would be a dangerous enemy to leave behind. She may be as dangerous as you are. Oh yes, I know you are inept and not too bright, but you are a dangerous enemy nonetheless, and she possibly even more so. You people hold grudges. Not a very nice trait—but you never let go, never give up. I wouldn't want her behind me the rest of my life. No more than I could sleep well at night, knowing you were still alive, looking for me."

"We have children, Baker. Two little girls. They need their mother. I'm begging you, for their sake."

"No. I'm sorry. Harlan, come over here." Ridgeway hurried across the room, raising the rifle to his shoulder and pointing it at me, eagerly. "No, Harlan, not yet. Put the rifle down. Damn it, put it down. We may need them yet. I'll tell you when. Now, I'm going to take Mr. Jacobs' car into Mannford and make a few telephone calls, to make arrangements for our departure." I want you to stay here and watch them to be sure they don't get away. But you are not to hurt anyone, you understand?"

I couldn't believe it. "Damnit, Baker, he's crazy. Don't leave him here alone with us. There's no telling what he'll do."

"Nonsense. He does what I tell him, don't you, Harlan? Besides, what difference will it make by this time tomorrow? It will all be over, and this will be behind us. You won't have another thing to worry about. None of you. Now, behave yourself Harlan, and I'll be back shortly."

He picked up my car keys from the table and left to make his calls. It occurred to me that apparently there never had been a phone at the cabin, and I felt a little less foolish about not looking for one the last time I had been there. I also got some satisfaction out of knowing Baker wouldn't find my own cell phone in the car. I had left it on the charger in my office.

Ridgeway watched him go, even moved to the doorway and watched the station wagon drive away. When the sound of the engine faded, he turned back into the room, walked over, and kicked me in the stomach again.

As I coughed and gasped for air, Ridgeway walked over to the couch and dropped onto it, laughing. He leaned the rifle against the arm of the couch, arched his back with his hands above his head, and stretched, and yawned heavily. "Man, am I ever tired. We have been going for three days straight now. I can feel my muscles starting to tighten up." He reached over and pulled Sherry toward him. She still had her back against the couch, with Ridgeway sitting on the couch behind her, his legs on either side of her shoulders. He leaned over and kissed her on the top of the head, all the time looking at me, watching my reactions. "I could sure use a little relaxation, you know? Some way to work out the kinks." He put his hands on the back of her neck, massaging her neck and shoulders. She looked at me, shook her head, and closed her eyes tightly. I could feel the bile rising in my throat from the anger and helplessness I was feeling.

Ridgeway laughed again and slid his hands down from her shoulders to cup each breast. Sherry shuddered and tried to twist away, but he pressed his legs against her sides, holding her in place. He pinched her nipples hard, and I could see tears of pain and anger on her cheeks.

"She doesn't like that. Not the way I do." We were all three startled to hear Joy's voice from the chair. Ridgeway jerked guiltily at the sound, like a small boy caught doing something he knew was wrong. Joy moved slightly in the chair. Her hands, taped at the wrists like Sherry's, began to push at the blanket until it slid from place and fell to the floor, leaving her uncovered and naked. "Why waste your time on her? She's old. She must be over thirty. And besides, like I said, she doesn't like it the way I do."

"You didn't like it this morning, you bitch! You fought me every moment."

"Of course I fought you, silly. Like I said, I like it rough. You got a little too rough, is all. You didn't have to punch me in the face like that. You messed me up. I must look terrible." She raised her tied hands above her head to fuss with her hair. The motion lifted her perfectly shaped breasts to attention, as she most certainly knew it would. She was baiting him. For a moment I wasn't sure whether she meant what she was saying, or if she was trying to distract him to protect Sherry. But when I saw the look in her eyes, I knew. Ridgeway was so far gone he might mistake that look for heated passion. I knew it was white hot hatred. She applied the final touch by arching her back and stretching out her long legs. It was too much for him. He rose to his feet, forgetting about Sherry, and moved quickly to kneel in front of Joy. He reached up to pull her from the chair down to the floor next to him. He rolled over on top of her, and I could hear her grunt from the weight. From the corner of my eye I detected motion, and when I looked back at Sherry she was sliding across the floor toward the fireplace. She managed to get up onto her knees and reach out with her bound hands to remove a fireplace poker from its stand. She then twisted until she could see that Ridgeway still had his back to her as he directed all his attention to Joy. Sherry began to crawl, roll, and slide her way across the ten or twelve feet toward Ridgeway. I kept trying to get her attention. I wanted her to come to me, to help me get loose while Ridgeway was preoccupied, but she ignored me. Finally she closed the distance, and moving quietly and deliberately, she pushed herself up onto her knees, moved just a little closer, then, clasping the fireplace poker in both hands, she raised it high above her head and brought it down on the back of Ridgeway's skull. He gasped, arched his back, and she hit him again. He groaned softly and collapsed.

Sherry sank back onto her heels, as Joy pushed up and rolled the bastard off, then turned over onto her side and curled up into a ball. Sherry dropped the poker and leaned over, trying to comfort her.

"Sherry, come on, sweetheart, get me loose before he comes to."

She rolled across the floor to my side.

"Reach under my shirt. The knife is hanging from a string around my neck." I had retrieved still another knife from my office safe. This one was another Italian switchblade, with a black handle and razor sharp stainless steel blade.

Sherry slid her hand inside my shirt and fumbled for the knife, grasping the handle and pulling down to break the string. I told her how to open the blade, and then rolled over so she could reach the rope around my wrists. In a moment I was free, and took the knife from her to free my ankles. Then I gently pulled the tape from her mouth, kissed her hurriedly, and used the knife to cut the tape from her wrists and ankles. After a quick hug she pulled away from me, started toward Joy, then reached back and took the knife from me. She hurried to Joy and started cutting her free.

Friends and Other Perishables

I stretched the kinks out, then moved over to check Ridgeway. He was still alive, but out cold. I dragged him back over to where I had been tied and used the same ropes to secure him. He would probably be out for quite a while, but why take chances? Crossing to Joy, I found she was conscious but possibly in shock. She was shivering and crying with her eyes closed and wouldn't respond to either Sherry or me. I picked her up and put her on the couch near the warmth of the fire. Sherry brought the blanket and covered her with it. She sat on the edge of the couch, trying to comfort the girl. I could see Sherry was crying, too.

"She did it for me. She distracted him so he would leave me alone, didn't she?"

"Yes, sweetheart, I think she did."

"After what that sick bastard had already done to her, she was willing to let him do it all over again. Carl, we've got to help her."

"We will, sweetheart, we will. Right now we have to worry about helping ourselves. Are you all right?"

Sherry suddenly realized she had been so concerned about Joy she hadn't thought about herself. "Oh my God, I must be a mess." She pulled the thin robe together to cover herself. As she buttoned it she remembered what had happened, glanced at me, and I was sure I noticed a slight blush, but I may have been mistaken. When she started messing with her hair I couldn't wait any longer. I pulled her to me and wrapped my arms around her. We stood like that for several minutes, gathering strength from each other. When Joy moaned softly, Sherry pulled away. "Enough of that silly stuff." She wiped her eyes dry. "Go get me some towels and warm water, and see if you can find some brandy somewhere."

I made sure Ridgeway was still out, then found my way

into the kitchen, where I ran a pan full of warm water and gathered up several towels from a rack near the sink. I carried everything back into the living room and set the pan on the floor next to the couch. Sherry immediately began to minister to Joy, speaking softly, encouragingly to her, and cleaning the blood off her face. I looked around some more and found the liquor in a corner cabinet. After pouring myself a stiff shot, I carried a glass and a bottle of very expensive cognac over to Sherry. I had noticed an empty scotch bottle in the cabinet and remembered what Baker said about Ridgeway getting into the scotch. Then I remembered Baker and the fact that he would soon be coming back.

"Sherry, how did they bring you here? Do you know what they did with their car? I didn't see it outside." I had decided it would be best to get the women away while we could and worry about catching Baker later.

"They hid it in a grove of trees a little further along the road. Maybe a few hundred yards. Andy said something about the police looking for it, and needing to hide it from helicopters, I think. He seemed pretty scared when we were driving up here. It was dark, and he must have been going a hundred miles an hour. A few times I thought we were going off the road. They're both crazy, Carl. Really crazy. I know Andy talks normally, sometimes, but don't expect him to act normally." She shook her head and shuddered slightly.

"Believe me, I won't, and he may be back any minute." Baker had taken my .45 and his own revolver with him when he left. I found my little Smith & Wesson lying on the table with my wallet and loose change. Dropping it into my coat pocket, I walked over and picked up Ridgeway's rifle. It was an excellent choice, a Remington bolt action .30-06 deer rifle. The bad part was that it had no sights. There was a mount for a scope, but no scope. The iron sights had been removed, or else the rifle was built without iron sights in anticipation of the scope. It was fully loaded, however, and I found an extra box of cartridges for it lying on the fireplace mantle.

I showed Sherry how to work the bolt, and showed her how to reload it if that became necessary. "I'm going out to get their car and bring it around. We'll take Joy and Ridgeway, and get the hell out of here. We'll let the police worry about catching Baker after you're safely out of the way."

I moved a chair up to a front window from where she could watch the road leading to the cabin, and told her if Baker showed up before I got back she was not to wait until he tried to get into the house. As he drove up, she was to start shooting at him, right through the window, and keep shooting until he left, or until she was out of ammunition. "Whatever you do, don't go outside. Stay in here and blast away. This thing will kick like a mule. Be sure to hold it tight against your shoulder. It doesn't have any sights, so you'll just have to point it and hope for the best. Besides, all you really want to do is scare him away."

"My daddy taught me how to shoot a rifle before he taught me how to drive. You worry about yourself, we'll be all right." She talked a good story, but I could tell she was nervous.

Outside the cabin the air was clear but cold. It was late afternoon, and the sun had set far enough to leave the road in the shadows of the tall trees lining each side. My breath formed an icy cloud preceding me along the road past the cabin. I moved quickly but had to slow several times to check out thick stands of trees just to make sure I didn't walk right past the car. I eventually found it, a late model Lincoln Town Car, dark green, and almost invisible in the shadows. As I might have expected, the damn thing was locked, and I had to break out a window to get inside. I searched in all the likely places, looking for an extra set of keys, but found nothing. I thought about that old stunt you see in the movies all the time where they rip out the ignition wires and touch a few of them together to start a car. I doubted it would ever work in real life, especially since I don't know a damn thing about cars or ignition systems, but since I didn't have any other ideas, I was lying in the floorboards reaching up under the dash to rip out the ignition wires when I heard the first shot.

CHAPTER FIFTEEN

I abandoned the useless Lincoln and ran back along the road toward the cabin. There were several more shots, a few I recognized as the crack of a deer rifle, followed by what sounded like a .38 Special. Andy was back.

As I got closer I heard the sound of my Buick station wagon starting up, and tires spinning on the gravel surface of the road. I rounded a turn in time to see the wagon backing away from the cabin at a high rate of speed, and saw the windshield shatter from still another round fired from the cabin. Sherry was better with the rifle than I had expected. Whether it was the shot or the spinning tires, I'm not sure, but Baker lost control of the station wagon, and I watched it back right off the road, bounce over the bar ditch, and smash into a large evergreen tree. After a brief pause, Baker opened the door and staggered out of the car. I raised the little .38 and fired two quick rounds, but the distance was too great. He ignored me, fired another round from his Colt revolver toward the cabin, then turned and ran into the trees. I started after him with every intention of running him down and tearing his head off, but just as I passed the cabin I heard Sherry scream.

Changing directions, I ran up the steps and crashed through the locked front door. The first thing I saw was Sherry, crouched on the floor beneath the windows, holding the rifle and staring in horror across the room. I turned my head and saw Joy. She was still naked, but there was nothing sensual about her now. Her breasts, stomach, arms, and hands were covered in blood. She was sitting astride

Ridgeway smiling down at him, her arms raised high above her head. As I watched, she drove her hands downward, plunging my switchblade knife into his chest for what must have been the tenth or twelfth time. His shirtfront was a mass of blood, and he was almost certainly dead after the first half dozen or so, but before I could move Joy stabbed him two more times and showed no sign of stopping anytime soon.

I finally managed to reach her and grab her wrists. She was surprisingly strong and resisted briefly, but when she looked up at me, then back down at what used to be Harlan Ridgeway, her face crumbled and she began to scream. I gathered her up in my arms and once again carried her over to the couch.

"Sherry, help me." Sherry dropped the rifle and moved toward us, slowly. She was still in shock from what she had witnessed. "Hand me the blanket, sweetheart." She picked it up and, instead of giving it to me, placed it gently over the hysterical girl herself.

While Sherry held Joy down on the couch, I crossed the room and picked up the roll of duct tape Baker had used on the women. I used some more of it to tape Joy's wrists together while Sherry looked on, disapprovingly. "Carl, is that really necessary?" I didn't answer, I just glanced over my shoulder at the bloody corpse at the foot of the stairs. Joy had stopped screaming but continued to moan and thrash around.

"Sherry, are you going to be all right?" I watched her closely, waiting for an answer.

"I'm okay, Carl. It was just so . . . I guess it was such a shock I lost it for a minute. I'm okay now, really." She looked in control again. Her voice shook a little, but I really didn't have any choice, anyway.

Friends and Other Perishables

"Sherry, I've got to go after him. He can't get far, not on foot. You stay right here and watch Joy. Don't take the tape off of her wrists under any circumstances. Even if she didn't hurt you, she might try to hurt herself. You understand?"

"Yes. I'm sorry, Carl, I didn't think of that. I'll be okay."

I handed her my revolver. "Here. It still has three rounds in it. He won't come back here, I know, but I'll feel better if you have it with you." I crossed to pick up the rifle, reloaded it from the box of cartridges and dropped the extra rounds into my coat pocket. At the door I paused only briefly and looked back. She was sitting on the edge of the couch, one hand holding the little .38, the other resting on Joy's forehead. She was watching me closely as I smiled, nodded good-bye, and stepped outside, pulling the splintered door closed behind me. It wouldn't lock, but there was enough of a door left to keep out the cold night air.

I half ran down the steps and crossed the gravel road, passing the station wagon, and started in the direction I had last seen Baker running. Not far into the trees I found that there was still enough snow on the ground to show footprints, and I picked up his trail almost immediately. Only a few yards further on, I found the Colt revolver lying in the snow. It was empty. A moment of exhilaration was followed by the realization that he still had my .45 automatic.

While I never pretended to be a modern day Daniel Boone, I had done quite a bit of hunting before I married Sherry, and I knew how to move through the trees with a minimum of sound, especially since the ground was soft and damp, and there were no dry leaves on the ground to rustle through. On the other hand, it was starting to get dark, and I didn't know my way around these particular woods. Since we had just left a cabin owned by Baker, I had to assume he was familiar with the area and knew where he was going. He left a trail through the snow that was easy enough to follow, even in the fading light, and as I thought about that, I recalled that old line again, from some "B" movie or other, when the hero looks particularly thoughtful and mutters to himself, "Almost too easy." And just about then Baker stepped from behind a tree and fired.

He had moved too soon, and I was too far away for the .45, especially since he wasn't familiar with the pistol. The slug whistled past my ear, and in reaction I dropped to the ground and rolled behind a tree, which I immediately realized wasn't nearly wide enough to hide behind. I pushed the rifle muzzle out in front of me, pointed the barrel in Baker's general direction, and fired. The loud crack was comforting, and even though the slug snapped off a limb at least four feet above his head, Baker acted as though he had found himself on a bull's eye. He lunged sideways, out of my line of sight, as I worked the bolt and fired again, hitting nothing as far as I could tell. The damn rifle was almost useless at this range, without sights. A moment later I heard him running through the brush. I jumped up, slipped in the snow a couple of times, lunged up again, and started after him.

He was able to move faster than me, primarily because he knew where he wanted to go, while I had to respond to the sounds he made and an occasional glimpse of his black overcoat flickering through the trees. About every fifty yards or so he would hide behind a tree or a rock and wait for me to come into range. Each time some sixth sense kept me from rushing out into open areas, and Baker simply wasn't a very good shot with a pistol. He was pretty good in the woods, though, but I was in better shape, and I knew if this went on for very long I would run him down. No such luck.

After only a few hundred yards, I came to another cabin. This one was small and dilapidated, and definitely qualified as a cabin. There was smoke coming from the brick chimney, and an old Ford pickup was parked under a lean-to off to one side. At first I thought Baker must have bypassed it, but the presence of the truck would have caught his attention. Transportation was probably what he wanted most right then. I moved toward the cabin, and once again a shot rang out and a .45 slug whistled just over my head. If he had had a little more patience, I would have walked right into it. As it was, I had time to drop into a gully out of sight before the next two rounds rang out.

As I lay there catching my breath, I tried to think back and count the shots Baker had fired. I also tried to remember whether he had taken the extra magazine with him or left it at the cabin. I couldn't remember seeing it lying with my wallet and other things, but then I hadn't really looked for it. If he had the magazine with him, he had started with fourteen rounds. If not, he had only seven when the shooting started, and I knew of at least six he had fired so far. One shot left or eight? That was quite a spread, and the difference could mean life or death. Something to think very hard about.

I also wondered about the occupants of the cabin. Baker hadn't had time to build a fire in the fireplace, so someone else must be inside. That could mean a hostage or two, and I hated the thought of that. I had to find out.

Studying the little gully I had dropped into, I saw that it curved around to the side of the cabin, getting gradually deeper as it turned downslope. It was rocky, and there had been water flowing over the bottom before the freeze. Now there were patches of treacherous ice I had to avoid as I moved along, keeping my head well below ground level, in an attempt to move around to a vantage point from where I could approach the cabin unobserved.

I only fell twice in spite of the fact that I was wearing hard-soled dress shoes and not hiking boots. My overcoat was warm enough, especially with the exertion of running through the woods to get here. I was perspiring under the coat, and I knew that before long, with little activity, I would start to get cold while Baker was warm inside the cabin. I was also very much aware that my bare hands, wet from the snow, were so cold I was starting to lose feeling in them.

I reached a point in the gully which placed a pile of cut firewood between me and the cabin. It was at the side of the cabin, and there was only one window on this side. Baker had apparently extinguished any lights that may have been in the cabin and the window was dark, but I could tell there was a white curtain over the opening, and it hadn't moved. That didn't mean someone inside wasn't looking out. Suddenly Baker made things much more simple.

"Jacobs, why don't you use your head? You've got no stake in this anymore. Your wife is safe, and I'm on the run. Just walk away. There's no sense in us killing each other." The sound of his voice came from the front of the cabin. He was calling out toward the spot where I had dropped to the ground. He didn't know I had moved.

"Come on, give it some thought. There's all that money back at the cabin. It's yours, now, if you let me go. Who's going to know? I'm damn sure not going to tell anyone. And Harlan won't talk if you threaten him. He's crazy, but he's also a coward. You can handle him, I know it." He sounded almost friendly.

I slid up over the rim of the gully and belly crawled toward the woodpile. When I snuggled up behind it, I was breathing heavily, and my breath was forming ice clouds which drifted upward, like a smoke signal pointing directly to my hiding place. I took time to pull my shirt collar up far enough to cover my mouth. The cloth helped to filter the moisture out of my breath and the signals stopped, at least momentarily. I was reassured when Baker started yelling again. His voice still came from the front of the cabin.

"Carl, damn it, let's talk, okay? Don't be so pig-headed. This is what I meant earlier when I said you held a grudge. Why take a chance? I just might put a bullet through you, you know. Then where would Sherry be with two small daughters to raise by herself? It's not worth that, is it? Give it up. Just walk away. You can tell them you tried to catch me, but I gave you the slip. No one would blame you for that."

I rose from behind the woodpile and moved quickly toward the cabin. When I reached the blind corner, I pressed my back against the wall next to the window and peeked around the corner. There was nothing to see for a moment, then suddenly Baker called out again. "Jacobs, damn it, don't be so anxious to die." And there, right in front of my eyes, a moist cloud of his breath drifted through a six inch gap at the bottom of the window, like an arrow pointing back at him, like a beautiful rainbow leading to my own golden reward.

I stepped around the corner, my back against the wall, held the rifle out at arm's length, horizontal to the ground, and spun to my right, driving the butt of the rifle through the opening, directly toward Baker's face. There was a satisfying thud from inside as he crashed to the floor. I glanced through the window and saw him sprawled on his back. I moved quickly to the front door of the cabin, but it was locked from the inside. Stepping back and lunging, I threw my considerable weight against the solid door, once, twice, and finally a third time before it gave, and I stumbled into the one-room cabin. The only light inside came from the fire in the fireplace. Turning toward the window I had to let my eyes adjust before I could see and realize Baker wasn't lying on the floor where he should have been.

He came up behind me from a dark corner of the room, his presence more felt than heard. He hit me with a chair and knocked me off my feet. I landed on my elbows, the impact driving the rifle from my hands and sending it skidding over the rough plank flooring to disappear under a bunk bed against the far wall. I rolled to one side just as Baker kicked out at the spot where my head would have been. I tried to roll once more but was stopped by the front wall of the cabin, my nose and chin bruised by the impact. Baker drove the toe of his shoe into my side, just above the kidney, before I could react. I was getting damn tired of being kicked.

I pushed myself away from the wall, reversing direction and rolling toward Baker, taking his legs out from under him. Not the best possible move, since when he fell, his knees drove into my chest, forcing the air from my lungs. While I was still gasping, he wrapped his fingers around my throat and began to squeeze. I wanted to breathe. All I could think of at that moment was that I had to inhale, and after that he could do what he wanted to with me. Just let me breathe.

I struck out. First with one fist, then the other. I couldn't see, but I knew where he was well enough. He was on top of me, and he had no intention of getting off. Again and again I struck wildly, finally driving both fists against his chest until he was forced back just enough. I raised one leg high, driving my knee up to my own shoulder, then drove my heel against his face, knocking him backward. He lost his grip on my throat as he tumbled head over heels, crashing into a shaky table, bringing it down on his head.

I gasped for precious air, filling my lungs as I scrambled to my feet. Now! Now it was going to be different. I was on my feet, my hands were free, and I was pissed.

I reached him before he could get to his feet. Locking my fingers onto the lapels of his coat, I pulled, twisting my body and lifting at the same time, tossing him cleanly over my hip. As he crashed to the floor, I lost my grip, and he rolled free, almost bouncing to his feet. The bastard was tougher than I had given him credit for, but he didn't seem very skilled. He came toward me, swinging roundhouse rights and lefts while he was still five feet away. His eyes were bright, glowing red from reflected firelight. Again he swung a right fist wildly, the force of the swing almost turning him completely around. Too late, I realized what was coming. He had deliberately put on the clumsy act to put himself in position for a spinning kick. As he spun to his left, his back almost to me, I saw his left foot leave the floor, his knee drawn almost up to his chest, and then his heel was driven into my side. I flew backwards, stumbled over a fallen chair, and crashed once again to the floor.

I managed to gain my feet before he was on me. He tried to press his advantage, this time with well-thrown punches, a straight right with all his weight behind it, followed by a left hook to my ribcage. I retreated, catching more blows on my forearms, or slapping them off-line, until finally he was slow following up, and I was able to throw a perfectly timed front snap kick, my hips square to the target, thrusting forward just like they teach you in dojos all over the world; and it worked. The toe of my shoe landed just above his beltline, and half of my foot seemed to disappear inside his gut. He folded and dropped as though he'd been shot.

I stood over him, breathing heavily, watching to see if he was going to get up. It looked like he was down for the count. I glanced around the room and spotted my .45 automatic lying on the floor beneath the window. The slide was open, and I thought at first it had locked back on an empty magazine, but when I picked it up and examined it more closely, I saw that a spent cartridge had become jammed in the breech, and instead of slapping the slide back, and removing the magazine to allow the casing to drop free, Baker had botched the job trying to force things. I pushed the magazine release and the nearly full magazine dropped into my left palm. I was switching hands, preparing to work the slide back to free the spent cartridge, when I heard him behind me.

I spun around and found Baker on his feet, advancing toward me, holding a ten-inch butcher knife. He held the knife in a very professional manner, point extended, flat of the blade horizontal to the floor, hand low and pulled back close to his hip, out of range of a defensive kick or desperate grab, but ready to thrust forward.

> *I know how to handle a knife . . . point extended, flat of the blade parallel to the ground . . . elbow close to the body . . . I remember, but I am afraid . . . alone . . . Jimmy ran away, left me . . . I want to run but I can't . . . the fat one, lying on the ground behind me . . . bleeding . . . screaming . . . his friend, the ugly one in front of me, shirt open, pants down around his ankles, reaching . . . slash across his belly . . . sharp point drawing a thin line of blood just above his navel . . . growing wider, and redder . . . him looking down, then at me, puzzled . . . shocked . . . afraid . . . of me? . . . run . . . run run runrunrunrunrunning . . .*

Friends and Other Perishables

★ ★ ★ ★ ★

I fumbled with the .45 as long as I could, but he reached me before I could clear the breech and insert the magazine. With surprising speed, he thrust the knife at my face, and in a purely reflexive move I leaned backward. That left my abdomen exposed to a sideways slash which would have gutted me if not for the heavy overcoat I still wore. As it was I felt the point of the knife cut through to the skin, and a moment later, I could feel the blood and my shirt sticking to my stomach.

Dropping the useless pistol, I continued to back away from him, occasionally bumping into things, until he backed me into a corner. I used my hands and arms to block him, as Baker jabbed and slashed, trying to force the blade through my defense. He seemed to grow stronger each time he drew blood from my hands and arms, as the sharp knife sliced through the sleeves of the coat. His eyes grew brighter, his lips drawn back in a grin, his breathing heavy and labored with exertion. I knew I couldn't continue like that for long.

Watching him closely, I could tell the moment he decided to end it. This time I was prepared for the thrust at my eyes. Instead of leaning backward away from the knife, I stepped into him, holding my left forearm across my body, and driving upward in a high-block, forcing the knife point up and to the side. The blade sliced along my wrist bone next to my watchband. With the same motion, I drove my right hand out, fingers held together, stiffly extended, pointing at his throat. Just as the point of the knife ripped through the edge of my left ear, my fingertips struck him below the chin, driving through and crushing the larynx. He fell to the floor, the forgotten knife still clutched in his right hand. He was gasping for breath which would never come.

He rolled over and over, making horrible sounds as he strangled on his own blood. It took a long time.

I was sitting on the floor, back against the wall, staring at his body when the door of the cabin opened and an elderly, bearded man carrying a shotgun and pair of skinned and gutted rabbits stepped inside. He looked around, mouth open, gawked at Baker's body, spotted me, then dropped the rabbits and raised the shotgun.

"What the hell is going on? Who are you and what're you doin' in my home?"

I shook my head. "It's a very long story, mister. But if that's your truck outside, I could sure use your help."

"Help, my ass. You just sit right there and don't move. I'm calling the sheriff."

"You've got a phone?"

"Well, hell yes. O' course I got a phone," he said, removing a cellular from his coat pocket. "Where you think you are, China?"

The old man took a lot of convincing, but after he had called the sheriff's office he eventually agreed to drive me back to Baker's cabin to make sure Sherry was all right. Before we left he pulled a tattered army blanket off the bunk in the corner and spread it over Baker's body.

He knew where to take me, because he remembered hearing shots from that direction earlier. He didn't investigate the matter, however, explaining that he had moved into the area in the first place because, around there "neighbors mind their own business."

As we pulled up in front of Baker's cabin, I could see Sherry looking out at us through the shattered window from where she had earlier driven off Baker with the rifle. Before we climbed the steps of the porch, she rushed out to throw her arms around me, ignoring the old man. He stood back, sort of shuffling his feet until she pulled away, giving me a chance to introduce them. "This is my wife, Sherry. Sherry, this is . . ."

"Howdy, Ma'am. My name's Brewster. Hank Brewster. I live back down the road a piece. Found your man in my cabin and brought him up to you. He needs more caring for than I could give him."

For the first time Sherry noticed the blood on my ear, and on my hands and arms, from the numerous cuts Baker had inflicted with the butcher knife. She almost started to cry but decided it wasn't the time and led me inside the cabin. Brewster followed us in, stopping just inside the door when he saw Ridgeway's body, then Joy lying on the couch. He raised the shotgun in a subconscious move of self-defense, then lowered it after glancing over to watch Sherry remove my coat and start to wash the blood off my arms.

"I thought one body was more than enough, and here I find you with two more. The sheriff's gonna be busy for a while on this case, I'll bet."

"The girl's not a body. She's just unconscious," Sherry said. Turning to me she continued, "She passed out shortly after you left. Where's Andy? Did you . . ."

I nodded my head, tiredly. "Yeah. He ran to Mr. Brewster's cabin and I caught up with him there. We had a fight, he came at me with a knife. I finally got lucky. He's dead, sweetheart." I looked over at Ridgeway, then back at her, eyebrows raised. She shook her head, glancing at Brewster.

I took the hint and turned to him. "Mr. Brewster, maybe you'd better go back to your place and meet the sheriff there. Then you can send him on up here. If you don't mind, I mean."

He glanced around once more. "That's okay by me. I think I'd rather wait outside anyhow. Ma'am, he's gonna need stitches in a few of those cuts. You'd best get him to a doctor when you can."

"I will. Thank you for your kindness, Mr. Brewster," Sherry called out, as he ducked his head a few times and backed out through the doorway, still holding his shotgun at the ready.

"Well, I see you've made a few changes," I said, as Sherry turned back to bandaging my hands with strips of cloth she had torn from something white. Looking across the room I could see that Ridgeway was no longer lying at the foot of the stairs, tied hand and foot, and tethered to the banister where he had been when Joy had killed him. He was now in front of the fireplace, with no ropes in evidence. His body was covered with a blanket, which peaked above the knife handle protruding from his chest. My knife. His right hand was sticking out from under the edge of the blanket, and clutched in his now stiff fingers was the fireplace poker Sherry had used on him. "What did you do with the ropes?"

She didn't look at me when she answered. "I put them in the fireplace. They made a horrible smell at first, with the blood and everything. I had to air out the room." She paused, then asked, anxiously, "It's okay, isn't it? With you, I mean? I know it's probably against the law, but damn it, Carl, she tried to save me from that bastard. She shouldn't be punished for killing him. She needs a friend right now, and after what she did for me . . . well, I want to help her, Carl."

Thinking about my own friendship with Jimmy Jay, I knew Joy wasn't the kind of friend I wanted my wife to have, but that wasn't a decision I could make for her. Besides, the decision had already been made.

"The police will be here any minute. What are we supposed to tell them? He swung the poker at her, so she stabbed him fifteen or twenty times? Do you think anyone's going to buy that?" I didn't really care if Joy got away with it, I just wanted to be sure we weren't caught in the middle.

"Carl, they'll believe whatever we tell them. We're respectable people, for God's sake. You're a private investigator, and I have a career, too, and I'm a housewife and a mother. Joy was visiting me, and we were kidnapped by these bastards, and you came and rescued us. That is what happened, after all. We'll keep it simple, and make it easy for them to accept. He was trying to rape and kill us, and Joy did what she had to do . . ."

I leaned back and closed my eyes as she went on laying out the story we would tell. I could get Sweet to help us put it over. He's an honest cop, but he's a good friend, too, and if he wouldn't think of doing it for me, he'd do it for Sherry and the girls. I knew it would work. Oh, they probably wouldn't believe us, but after Sherry built up a head of steam and presented her side of things, who was going to cross her? Not me.

About the Author

Dale Whisman is uniquely qualified to write about the world of private investigators. He was a licensed Private Investigator for eleven years, working as an Insurance Fraud Investigator with a company known throughout the four-state area of Oklahoma, Texas, Arkansas, and Kansas for their success in obtaining video tape evidence to combat fraudulent injury claims. In addition to conducting surveillances, he also investigated instances of suspected arson, product liability, theft, and missing persons. Dale is trained in Karate, and has won several trophies in combat pistol competition. He resides in Tulsa, OK, with his wife Sherry. They have two grown children, and six grandchildren.